Lost on the Way Home

Schuster Hill Chronicles

Johnathan R. Patrick

Copyright © 2020 Johnathan R. Patrick

All Rights Reserved.

ISBN 978-0-578-66653-2

Editing by Mike Valentino

Proofread by Bettye Rideout

Printed and bound in the United States

Published by JP Productions, PLLC

Instagram: @JP.Write

Email: Johnathan@JPWritesProductions.com

For God,

Thanks for Everything, Seen and Unseen.

For My Crew,

Thanks for the frustrations, the love, the laughs, the meltdowns, and all the Everythings. I couldn't have made it this far without you helping me to be crazy behind my Dreams.

A lamp unto my feet and a light to my pathway is He to me.

There I stood amid this autumn evening trying to make some sense of what I was witnessing. Mrs. Ramirez was all over the place carrying on in a way that, in any other context, would have caused suspicion. Nonetheless, there I stood trying to get her to calm down and speak English, but it was like trying to push a string up a hill; the very fabric of her existence had torn wide open and was seeping out. I could only witness her cry. What a horrific ordeal -- her child disappearing from the playground outside of their home. Hell yeah, she's literally forgotten all her English. It wouldn't surprise me one bit if the woman started speaking in some long-since dead tongue. Who could possibly blame her?

While the police spread around her property like a disturbed ant colony, I was witnessing her literal death. It is baffling to know that in a town with such an affluent population of Spanish migrant workers, not one officer in sight could even begin to try understanding what she attempted to explain. I am translating her every word in my head, but my mouth can't speak. She and I really aren't much different. We are both mothers, and just like twins, her pain runs deeper than the heart can reach. It has tapped her soul, and though I don't stand in her shoes, I feel the deep hurt of this excruciating pain. My thoughts traveled to far stretches, but then my soul couldn't take it anymore. I know this young man didn't deserve my mouth, but the breath of another mother's plight had to fill in for my sister. After all, he's the rookie cop from the newspaper, and this moment will someday be looked back on as one of those good character-building experiments. I'm still wondering why he would be on a solo mission taking this mother's statement with no direction from a more seasoned officer. Why wouldn't the Chief of Police be here? The why's of it all makes this whole situation even shittier than it needs to be. This young man was at his wit's end. I could tell it from his face. It was time to do something different.

"Stop! Just Stop it!" I shouted at him. "This woman is traumatized. Can't you see the fucking trauma oozing from her body? She can't calm down! All she knows is that her baby is gone. He should be there on that damn swing set. Her being calm isn't important anymore. Stop treating her like a god-damn suspect and find her son! Just tell your Chief that we're on our way to the station."

I was hopeful that going to the actual police department and meeting with the Chief would do justice a solid. It's a 20-minute drive, and that might be enough time for me to try and talk with Mrs. Ramirez. God knows I don't want to imagine what she is feeling on the inside, but each time I glanced over at her, I saw flashes of my son snatched. All week I had been having silent regrets of sending my son Remi to Seattle with Uncle Buck, but in times like these, I'm glad to know my baby is in great hands and not here in this place.

The ride to the station was so tranquil. I put Mrs. Ramirez in the car like she was Remi, strapped her in the seat, and made sure she was comfortable all without suggesting words. I was hoping there would be some encouraging thoughts that would come to mind, so I took the country road eight and made it a 30-minute ride considering the ridiculous potholes. For just a quick moment, I was reminded that I needed to raise hell with the County Judge. These streets look and drive as the highway of a Third World country rather than midtown rural Texas. As we drove the road, I glanced over at her sobbing silently. It occurred to me that she was alone. Her son is all she had here; she is a long way from her family in Puerto Rico. At this moment in time, I'm all she has. As we traveled down the road silently, there was this huge thud from my front right tire. It sounded like a blowout. That thud was all it took to get her to scream and start sobbing profusely and sharply. I snatched the car to the side of the road to make sure, but her crying was like a sharp nail piercing my brain slowly. I could barely handle it.

Christ, the Lord Jesus, knows I know that it is from a place of deep pain, but I grabbed her hand and squeezed tightly while looking into her pain-stricken eyes.

"Mrs. Ramirez, I know the last thing you want to hear is calm down, but Honey, you just got to do it. These police don't give a damn about little Raphael, and they are looking for any little reason to discharge his case. He's 14, and they are going to ask you all these questions about his happiness at home and school. And when they get tired of claiming you're a suspect in this case, they are going to discount it as he ran away. I'm new to this community, but I grew up with this kind of disparity on the daily in my hometown. I've not known the police ever to work hard to find any child that isn't privileged and white. And another thang, you can't keep screaming in my ear like that. I love you dearly, but I'll have to put you on the back of this truck if we can't pull it in."

I don't know if she processed anything else, but that last part made her start laughing so hard and long that I just knew the woman had lost it. I was thinking, oh my sweet Jesus, how am I going to fix this now! But when the laughter stopped, she dropped my hand and got to tunneling through her purse and pulled out this little gold foiled invitation envelope with a wax seal on the back. She asked if we should open it. With quick thinking about some deadly powder spewing out and killing us, I said "no" and snatched the car into gear, and we zipped to the police station. Before getting out of the car, I grabbed her hand again and looked her into the eyes and said, "Remember what I said. Do your best to play calm and speak in English. I'm here for you; worry about nothing else. Just know I got you."

We entered the building. I looked around and found the seat closest to the "police personnel only" sign and noticed that her legs were trembling. She was coping at her best. Just a few feet away was the police clerk's window. What a real slob of a woman she was. She sat her rude self up there, primping and frowning as if I was disturbing her best life. All the while looking at me like I was crazy and started barking, "What you want, and if you are looking for the Chief, he ain't here." And the woman slammed the glass window shut. The very idea of remaining calm became a mere afterthought.

"The name's Lucy Sanchez and my friend's son has been abducted, so what I need is for you to tell Chief Marcelle to get his ass in gear and get here pronto. Is that clear enough for you, Honey-Chile."

Unfazed by my plight, she again looked up and over those lime green-winged tip glasses and said, "There was a murder on 31st Street down by the Mayor's house! I'm indeed sorry to hear about your friend's child. The Chief is aware that you're here, Ms. Lucy, and he'll be here soon as he can."

At that point, I felt two inches tall. Not to say the murder overshadows Raphael, but it is equally important. I took my seat beside Mrs. Ramirez, and we waited for about 20 minutes, and the Chief entered the front door. On sight, he knew who we were and approached us with a true look of concern for the situation.

We entered the office fully expecting to get some understanding and a hint of solace for this whole situation, but what we got was more of the same from earlier tonight times 20. This time she was subjected to interrogation about her entire family life. Her child was missing, but her husband, who was on the run and wanted for murder, seemed like the Chief's only interest. She had no answers to his whereabouts. Her legs were again shaking, but her voice remained clear and without rattle. She sat there looking at the Chief squarely in his eyes and spoke boldly.

"Look, I get it...you think my husband did something terrible and got away with it. He's gone, and quite frankly, I don't care about him right now. Now my baby is lost, might be dead or he might be in somebody's damn basement. Just for the sake of this moment, let's pretend that his life matters."

I looked at her and then back at the Chief and then again in her direction. In my mind, I was saying *that's my girl right there*. I now understood why little Raphael was always so quiet. The child had to walk in the shadow of his father's alleged wrongdoings, all the while pretending to be invisible so that he wouldn't bring any more attention to his family. She didn't need my input, but I had to cosign.

"Enough with the questions of her husband and his tragic fate. What's at hand now is her 10-year-old son has gone missing from her backyard, and the only thing that was left behind besides her memories is this damn gold foiled envelope."

"By the way, open it," he said, "Miss, umm…"

"The name is Lucy Sanchez."

"Indeed, you're the one running that youth center. From what I hear, the kids are thriving."

"Chief, we can discuss how great my foundation is doing at a later hour. Right now, we need you to take this poor lady's experience seriously. Her child was abducted, and the sick bastard left this souvenir behind."

He sat there looking almost intrigued that these two women were sitting here demanding his attention. Reaching for the envelope, I flicked it onto his desk. I asked if he had indeed seen this before in any prior case. He cut me off swiftly.

"No, ma'am, this is my first time seeing anything like this, and it appears to be wax sealed." He pushed a button on his phone and told the cocky clerk to get a guy in a hazard suit into the examination room. We were ushered into a place that you usually see on TV where the witness picks a suspect out of a line-up. Before long, a man showed up in a hazardous waste jumpsuit and broke the seal of the envelope. No *toxic* waste or huge black spider jumped out to kill him.

Mrs. Ramirez again found her way to my hand like that of a small child, fearing the boogeyman. I looked down at her leg and noticed they were starting to buckle. Her eyes appeared swollen, no doubt from the crying and wiping away of tears. I felt ashamed that what I was presently doing was all I could do for her situation. The guy behind the glass window approached it closer and pulled out a blood-red invitation that read, "he's been here." I still can't explain it, but when she read those words, she lost it. The woman went to screaming at the top of her hoarsened lungs.

"Raphael Raphael, my poor baby!"

"Father! My Baby, My Baby!"

The Chief stood there through the whole scene and did nothing but wear that damn annoying smirk. Finally, when I glanced his way, he hit another button, and a paramedic came rushing into the room. It became apparent to me that she could not be alone and needed a means of relaxation that I couldn't provide her. They struggled with her jolting and trying to run away for a few minutes. I saw utter fear in her eyes. I guess the rehashing of her husband's fiasco and now a missing child must have made something snap in her mind. This had to be one of the most frightening moments of my life. And I was raised in South-Central LA. My heart pulsated like granny's old sewing machine when she started screaming my name and reaching in my direction.

"Ms. Lucy, please don't let them take me. Please! Please don't let them take me away. I won't make it."

"I'm right here! You have nothing to worry about; these folks are just going to help you relax and get some rest. I'll be right over in the morning to pick you up. We're going to get through this and bring your baby home. I promise."

My voice was like the light to her pathway in calming down. She got quiet and seemed to have gained assurance that all was going to be well. But when they got her to the door, she stopped, looked back and screamed, "He's Been Here!" and she fainted and they had to carry her to the ambulance. I followed them outside and watched as they got her loaded and strapped in the back of it. I glanced over my shoulder and saw the Chief glaring at me from the station door. I didn't know what to think of the man at all. His calm created a considerable pause. He never once tonight said that we are going to do our best to find your son. It's like he knows that this is a lost cause, and he is entirely at peace with it all.

The minute I got inside my home, I had the eeriest feeling of fear fall upon me. I kept brushing it off and telling myself it's just the jitters. But every time I tried getting to sleep, I heard her voice shrieking the message from the invitation

"He's been here! HE'S BEEN HERE!"

I couldn't put my finger on it, but something didn't sit right. I tried all that evening to get to sleep, but fear got the best of me. I lay in bed wondering to myself why does tragedy always seem to find a home near me? I looked over at my evening meds and got ready to start a private pity party but just flipped the Monday cap and downed a bottle of water, and before long, I was fast asleep. I dreamed of traveling the streets on a love seat and visiting a friend's home and being slapped to the floor by a little boy and almost raped by my friend's husband.

I woke up to a brand new morning in a deep cold sweat, not knowing what to think of what I had just endured in the dream world. Mrs. Ramirez hit my mind, and I started barreling out of bed to get myself prepared to pick her up from the hospital. I skipped breakfast at home so that she and I could sit down together for a plate of Big Larry's flapjacks and come up with a game plan. Only there would be no flapjacks this morning and no pondering through a game plan. Worst of all, there was no living Mrs. Ramirez. I was told she had a severe reaction to the meds administered to her for rest and went into Anaphylactic shock and couldn't be revived around midnight last night.

I stood there in the hallways of the historic hospital, just not making any sense of this whole matter. What are the odds of the woman being allergic to Benadryl? Who the hell dies at a time like this? She has no one here but I, and I don't know of any next of kin to contact. Her remains will be sent to the state to be cremated like a Jane Doe if no one steps up to claim responsibility. I waited a week to give the mysterious figures time all the while, knowing no one would come forward for the dear soul. Just like her son, only I remained to give a damn for her now. I contacted Schuster Hill Funeral Parlor on the outskirts of town; from what I heard, the ladies take great pride in their work. Their mission statement read, "working fast together to make your last viewing better than your first sighting." I went through the formalities with Big

Slim, and when we were just about done, her daughter Ellis entered the office, and we got a chance just to talk and get to know each other. They were down to earth, well to do black women who were secure in their position in life and put off no airs either way. Classic Women are they. When everything was completed, Big Slim invited me to walk up the hill to the grand ole mansion she shared with her widowed daughter and four grandsons. Ellis' husband died a few years back in a head-on collision motorcycle accident at the hands of a drunk driver.

I got busy at the foundation and didn't have the opportunity to view her body until the day of the funeral. Nonetheless, their reputation definitely proceeded them. Mrs. Ramirez looked as if she were merely sleeping. The first two front rows were reserved for any family members that might have shown. Overall the community, as well as the families of every participating youth from the foundation, were present. The room seated 250 people comfortably, and much to my surprise, it was filled. I don't know how the spiritual world operates, but if she were allowed to check-in, I'm sure her soul would be significantly warmed by the outpouring of attendees there to celebrate her life. They did a magnificent job of directing the service. Ellis and Big Slim trained those four little fellas well. The little ones with the oldest being about twelve and the triplets about ten handled seating and everything in between while their granny commanded that Hammond organ and those twin tallboy Leslie speakers with their mother on the piano both duking out the musical tones like classically trained maestros. They tag-teamed songs like "I Shall Wear a Crown," "Everyday Should be A Day of Thanksgiving," and just oh my God when Sister Aria made the organ voice out "Jesus Precious King" and she and Ellis took turns belting from heights unknown there wasn't a dry eye in the place except for their little ones. They no doubt got a chance to hear this grand pleasure on the daily. The service lasted for about 45 minutes, and let me tell you it was 45 minutes too short. I, in my whole life, had never encountered anything so beautiful as this service. Everything went smoothly. The music was fit for a queen meeting her king. They had to have been trained by angels and reared in the anointing and perfected by the Holy Ghost Himself for just this moment in time. Her remains were interred at the family cemetery behind the funeral parlor. When the last hand was shook, and no more hugs stood to be embraced, Big Slim came to me.

"Baby, was everything to your liking?"

Still blown away by their presentation, I thought to myself I wish I could die right now to do this all over again. But the hands of the copper-toned blue-eyed mangling gray hair lady aided my escape from Lala land with a swift shake.

"Child, come on back to the right now."

"Yes. Yes, ma'am! You all have been simply beautiful."

She smiled and walked me to my car.

"Child, you take care of yourself. I want you to know that you got our vote."

I didn't understand, but I went with the flow. "Thank you, ma'am. Thanks for everything."

"It was our pleasure, baby. But one other thing, you be careful down there in Schuster's Landing, nothing and I do mean nothing is it what it seems. God created them with good intentions, but fear paired with a well-meaning person can be lethal for people like you and I. I rise before the rooster, but he beats me to bed. So, if you ever need Big Slim, just call."

With no further words, we parted ways. In my rearview, I took pleasure in seeing the estate fade into the distance. The drive from Schuster Hill to Schuster's Landing is about 15 miles on old County Road 8. The potholes demand respect for the jaded pavement queen and provide time to think things over. About five miles down the road, I was met by Chief Marcelle Carraway sitting in his black Chevy Tahoe on the side of the road as if he were waiting for my return. For some reason, I expected him to flag me down, but instead, the dark-eyed fellow just glared into my car at me wearing what I would determine to be his look. I have to admit he makes my spine echo chills, but I won't be afraid of him; after all, he's just a man. Raphael flashed across my mind and caused me to slam the brakes and snatch the car in reverse like a stunt driver.

"Hey, where are we on the Ramirez case?"

"Well, good evening to you too, Ms. Lucy."

"Evening, do you have any updates? It's been weeks now, and no one has provided me with anything. His mom is gone, and I'm hellbent to bring this child home. Do you have anything?"

"How noble of you, but like I said last week, when I know more, you'll know more, Ms. Lucy."

Somehow, I always manage to wake up ten minutes before my alarm starts dinging, it's almost like I command myself to defeat the thing. Turning into my mother, no doubt. The woman never needed a clock to tell the time. It was like she had become one with time. There's so much to get done at the center this week. The summer session is now over, and this is the first week of the fall semester. My permanent staff of five full-time workers has done a great job so far. I couldn't ask for a better team. They've impressed upon me their sincere devotion. The university will be sending over a new round of about 20 volunteers. We held interviews during the last two weeks of July. It's kind of funny that I said "we" when I left it all in the hands of the crew.

Miss Raychelle heads the tutoring department.

Miss Sadie is the music department.

Mr. Theodore is the health and fitness department

Mr. Reilly, STEM Department

Reggie is my assistant and the office manager

All play a role in mentoring and head a team of the college volunteers. Only one of the best teams a leader could ask for. Tis foundation strives to be unlike any other after school program in the region. The center focuses on the total education experience. Every couple of Saturdays, we offer enrichment programs where we bus the kids to the inner city to discover and explore science museums, the theater, and music concerts. This program has become a real pillar of the community's youth, and their parents are involved as well. The foundation has been in the city for almost a year and a half now. Not a day goes by where we don't get word of praise from somewhere.

The planning meeting felt sort of stuffy. The air was thick. Usually, this is one of the liveliest teams you'd ever meet. Jokes bounce off the walls like rubber balls. But today things are just too quiet for comfort but for good reasons. I know where everyone's hearts and minds are. I can still see their faces yesterday. I need to address this, but the truth is, I'm at a loss for words. I took my seat at the head of the conference table and peered down at the end of the table to Reggie and then channeled around the table counterclockwise at every sober set of eyes all the while I ran four flats in search of the right words.

"Guys, our mission statement says that we are the one-stop youth transformers."

I felt the frog starting to leap in my voice, but I pressed forward. "I know where your hearts are, and I'm right there with you. But we will get through this. Raphael's fate is depending on our Faith to get him back safely. God can't rest Mrs. Ramirez's soul until her son is back safe within the hearts of our love. Now we have the task of not only doing our jobs but also being investigators into his case. Now tell me, does this envelope hold any significance to anyone?"

Both Miss Sadie and Miss Raychelle gasped in fear and got a severe case of the big-eyed disease. Raychelle screamed, "Sweet Jesus, no, no, not that!" She burst into tears and bolted to the door. With the men trailing behind her fleeing steps, Sadie just stayed planted in her seat with her head down and mumbling to herself.

"Miss Sadie, Sadie, what is this a sign of?"

"Evil people with money playing God, Ms. Lucy. You know Sadie and I are first cousins, right?"

"Yes, ma'am."

"About 15 years ago when we weren't but like 12 or 13 years old, they called us the three musketeers until Margie went missing. From how I came to understand it, her parents always had financial issues. Mostly because her dad was a terrible gambling addict and just an all-around worthless bucket of flesh. They were close to getting evicted out the little shack they called home, barely had food to feed the kids, and were using candles to light the house. Aunt Margaret worked for the Grubbie family, so she went out on a limb and asked for a loan. My mom said Mrs. Grubbie slapped the spit out of Aunt Margaret before she could even finish asking. She started laughing like a mad lady and sent for her husband, by the way, the servants. I can't remember any of the real specifics of that scene, but they ended up sending Margaret and Uncle Riley to see some strange white folks that no one knew, and after that night, things appeared to have gotten better for them. Hell, they had something to spare my family for a while. They weren't financially stricken anymore. Aunt Margaret quit her job, and Uncle Riley continued to do his usual gambling routine. Then some months later came a stormy night; aside from the thundering you heard the horses hitting the water and saw the lights of the lanterns in the hands of what appeared as the Klan. You know black folks back then didn't fool with the Klan, so of course, no one tried to see anything. Uncle Riley knew to come outside and wait to be called. He might have been shy of one more step to the muddy ground when the shot was heard, and his lifeless body hit the ground. They rode off with no further actions. I don't know, but maybe two or three weeks later, Margie was outside helping her mom hang clothes on the line when Aunty went back inside for more clothespins and when she returned, there was no hint of Margie other than what you pulled out of your purse a few minutes ago. From that time till now, Margie never resurfaced. We know not whether she is alive or dead.

"If Raphael is in the hands of that fate, he too won't be found. Ms. Lucy, this ain't no time to play damn Nancy Drew or spying with your middle eye. But if that's what you got in mind, let me know, and we'll quit this job today. You can't fight a battle when your opponent wears the face of many unknowns. They don't mind killing you. Look at what happened to Mrs. Ramirez. Please promise me right now you'll forget about anything attached to that envelope. I know you care for them, but it is beyond our hope. We do a great job here, and I promise you if noise gets around the town of you snooping around pushing this issue, they got a way of ringing your doorbell and baby by the time you hear the bell it's too late. We all have families here, and as much as we loved and treasured little Raphael and his mom, we can't join them so quickly. Now let us go check on Sadie, and remember what I said, Miss Lucy. I'll make something up for the men, and you just follow my lead."

I stood there in silence with the horrors of this past and present-day situation flashing through my mind. I had no choice but to give her my word to let this go.

We went about our duties as if the incident of today had been erased. I sat around my office, silently trying to string it all together. I know that someone is abducting children as a means of debt collection. I know the struggle is real, but is it ever really enough to bid your children goodbye for a few moments of financial peace? The very thought of this invisible evil had me really looking over my shoulders. I've been here for a while now, and up till this point, I never knew a thing. The occurrences over the last two weeks have really shaken my soul. It's not the dying that worries me, although I'm not interested in death, just the thought that people are financially distressed enough to knowingly put their family's life in jeopardy. Just for a temporary come up, they have no problem writing their children and possibly themselves out of the scene. They must have it in their minds that they don't want to see their children suffering, but damn, stop and think this thing clear. I wanted to talk more with both Miss Sadie and Miss Raychelle, but that's not an option. Raychelle gave me a glimpse into this thing, but her words "you don't know who is involved and they don't mind killing," really stood out. I really don't know who to trust, and

I don't want anyone getting hurt because of my curiosity. I told myself you can let this go; you can forget it happened. Maybe I can, but can I is the real question. I know I can't make this thing go away, but I can't afford to be stupid either.

This is the first day of the fall session, and time is really ticking away. In less than an hour, half this building will be brimming with little people. I need to call Mrs. Pringlaye over at Sandwich Express to let her know I'll be there in a few to pick up those delicious sandwiches. Amid all this drama, I still got to see how blessed I am. Pringlaye's business rotates meal donations with two other businesses (Jaden over at Tasty Express and Mr. Richmond at Slap-Da-Tongue BBQ) that have been committed to the program since its inception. Feeding our nearly 200 participants and volunteers has been as easy as ordering takeout. I really can't ask for a better set of supporters around town, just about everything the program has needed has practically been donated. This high expression of generosity allows me to pay my workers respectable salaries.

"Hey, Reggie. I'm headed to Sandwich Express, give me four copies of the meal schedule for this session. I'll give everyone their copies before picking up the meals from Mrs. Pringlaye."

"Ms. Lucy, let me do that for you. You already do too much."

"You on the outside of this building means the children won't get fed, and I don't think you want to be fired today."

"Jesus! Fire me! Lord, I forgot one small thing almost a year ago, and you still trying to behead a brother. You'd think I goof off all the time."

"Sir, pass me those keys off the wall. You're right; it was only about 200 hungry children, pissed off staff

17

members, and livid parents. Small potatoes, huh? You are truly something else. And you know I know you on that phone with Bella Fontae, right?"

"Bye, Felicia."

"Yeah, I got your Felicia, that's what they'll be telling you at the Unemployment office. Slip up, and you going to fall, Sir."

This little character really makes my day. Indeed, he is a natural fool, but he does such a great job even with his personal phone attached to his face at all times. When we have our pre-morning conference meetings, I make sure to speak to his best friend, Miss Bella-Fontae. He always laughs me off and swears he's not on the phone and then whisper "gotta go." Nonetheless, a real stand-up guy, a little catty, but that comes with the territory of being him.

Not only am I blessed, but I am so blessed. The three donor restaurants are next door to each other. Upon entering each business, I feel like I'm on the set of Cheers. Whenever I feel down and out, I just make my way downtown and love for Ms. Lucy is everywhere. Jayden, a beautiful mixed-race black/Chinese man, is always especially glad to see me. He is just too pretty to be a man….his masculinity is always on fleek. Since I moved to town, he has made Remi and me his special interest. There is always a private table in his office waiting for us that I am ashamed to admit I indulge at least three days a week on weekdays and always on Sunday. But before I get judged, I do give back, just not with what Jayden would love to accept. Just another checkmate of being HIV Positive. I'm blessed that my little man didn't contract the disease through birth, but I'll never know love with my dream man because of this sad reality.

I would love to fall deeply in love with this man. My spirit always tries to get me to come clean with him and just see where the cards will fall, but my fear can't put his health in jeopardy. I just know he would gladly marry me even on my worst day. He's a real gentleman, an excellent listener, and selfless. Just last summer, during the summer retreat, the participants requested that he cater to the summer session feast, and despite my best efforts, he refused to charge us. I just felt like his kindness was too much, and I needed to pay him for his service, but what can you say to a man that refuses to accept your token. I thought I would be smart and have Mr. Harry from the church donate to his business, but as of yet, he hasn't cashed the check. A solution always abides in his soul. I wish there was one for my situation. I had some time to spare while Pringlaye's staff loaded the meals in the van, and after eating a couple of her new almond flour crusted hoagie sandwiches, I needed to walk around, or I was going to need a nap. The woman has got to be lacing these sandwiches with crack or something. Whew, Chile! The other meal schedules still need to be delivered to the others, so of course, I stopped by Jayden's first and just as soon as I darted through the door it all began.

"Ms. Lucy" rang around the room from all notions of the tongue. At any given moment, you'll find people of just about any race visiting us here in Schuster's Landing, the locals call it the original melting pot. As usual, Jayden ushered me into his office, snatched the schedules out of my hand, and dashed over to the door. He made a 360 back to the door.

"Hey, Lil Girl, I'll be back in a minute." His voice is just so velvety smooth I could just melt in his arms.

Within a few minutes, he'd be back. In the meantime, I just stood and did what came naturally, clearing and rearranging his desk. I can hear him now saying, "Umm, ma'am, how many times have I you told to leave my stuff be? I got a system in here that you mess up every time you stop by. Let my office look like a man works here." Just as I was putting on the finishing touches, he appeared standing in the doorway, just smiling.

"How you doing, Sir?"

"Oh, really, you gonna act like you didn't just mess up my desk system? But we ain't gone talk about that. I'm better now that the Queen of my Heart is here destroying my office."

We just burst into laughter. He blushes harder than a clown's red nose.

"Well, hello to you too, Mr. Arnold," I offered while looking puppy doggish.

"Don't come in here with that puppy in heat look, mess around and be my wife. I was here waiting on somebody to show up yesterday evening with this certain schedule. What happened? Oh, yeah, I think Mr. Richmond says you ain't been showing him no love."

"How can I when you insist on delivering the schedule every month?"

"I told that ole cat you my woman. What I look like letting you be down there, letting him hug all that old spice on ya clothes?"

"You just too much, now I gotta go smooth things out with Mr. Richmond. But you know, after Mrs. Ramirez's funeral, I just went home, ate, and went to sleep. I was drained."

"That's right. I forgot all about that, did everything go well? Was any of her family able to attend?"

"Everything went well, and no, her family wasn't able to attend. But listen, I want you to come by the house this week whatever day is good for you. We need to talk."

"I'm free tonight, Ms. Lucy. What time do I need to be there? What the hell we finna do this time, paint the house? Don't say a word; I'll bring some food. I can see this going to be a long-ass night."

"Cool, make sure to bring my favorite."

He scoffed, "Ain't nobody bringing all that damn food. I swear you're the fittest but the hungriest little woman I ever met. I know Mrs. Pringlaye done fed you with one of them damn hoagies."

Mrs. Pringlaye texted me, letting me know the meals were loaded. I left his office feeling happier than when I'd entered. As I closed the door, he yelled, "Aight, I'll see ya tonight, Queen!"

While sitting at the stoplight, I thought to myself, "those damn hoagies, though."

Each session starts out just about the same as the one before it, however this one is a bit different. Yes, it is just pretty much an evening of meeting and greeting the students, parents, center facilitators, and volunteers. The only thing different now is I'm expecting some phantom of the dark opera to start snatching kids and killing randomly. Thankfully, overall, everyone has had a good time so far. In this session, we gained 25 new enrollees who surprisingly all desired to be a part of both the theatre and dance programs. These programs allow us to further enrich the minds of the children to think outside of the standard x plus y equals this mindset. After all, these are our future leaders of tomorrow. I say there were no incidents, but there was a surprise in our midst. Ten-year-old Silas Harley, son of Chief Marcelle Harley, happened to be one of the newcomers.

At first sighting, the young fella's face caught my attention most of the evening, but I just couldn't place his familiarity. Then by the close of the evening, it all became clear. Of all parents and of all children, he had to belong to him. I didn't know the man even had children much less would ever think to enroll them at my center. Why on earth would he have his son attending Eagle Side Elementary, highly improbable? I didn't want to really cross paths with the Chief, but I got myself mentally prepared for the inevitable. Personally, I have no real reason to hate him, yet I really have no reason to trust him either. Our last encounter wasn't the best. I'm a bit fearful of how this one might develop.

The enrollment table was nearly out of enrollment forms. A perfect excuse for me to slip off to my comfort spot. Once there, of course, there was a light knock at the door. It seemed a bit too quiet for who I thought it to be, considering he's inclined to kick doors off the hinges. I looked over my right shoulder, and of course, it was my date. There was never a time when I wanted to see Jayden more than right now. I bolted to the door like a crazed 16-year-old virgin smiling and gushing while my heart's one beat felt like that of a thousand.

"I saw Marcelle walking from this way, did you get a chance to talk to him?"

I didn't see him, but I felt his presence in my spirit. I knew he was near. "No, he didn't come in here, probably was looking for little Silas. He's such a handsome little fella."

"Yeah, thank God he took on features of his sweet mother, God rest her soul. Cause that cat he calls father is a real skillet, one of those old ugly cast iron caked up grease skillets."

"I get it, shut up, everybody can't be the prettiest man in a town like you, my dear homie."

Before the last word rolled off my tongue, I knew I had struck a nerve. He immediately became silent. The one thing any man resents is to be called is pretty, and this man can catch an attitude quicker than a cat can lick its ass. I can push his button probably worse than his mother, and even worse, I enjoy doing it. But I promise this was not a moment where I was trying.

"Jayden, lighten up. My God, you act worse than those the darker complexed brothers who hate to be called black, you are a gorgeous sexy man that half of the town wants. Now bring your pretty ass here and give Queen Lucy a hug."

He stood there looking at me, no smile, no words, and didn't move; I had to walk to him and take my hug. I knew he couldn't be that pissed that quick either, but I'd play along for the sport. I wrapped my arms around him and whispered in his ear, "Jayden, I'm sorry. I'll never call you pretty again. But I should be punished for even thinking such word applies to you." Pressing my breasts closer to his chest, I asked, "You forgive me, right?"

"Yeah, yeah, you deserve to be punished, just know when I strike it hurts, little girl."

"Girl? Little Girl? Really? There's a lot of them outside, but I know you couldn't be referring to Lucy Sanchez." It was now my turn to act pissed.

"You know what? Get out of my office. And I still win this round. A pup can't play me, little player, I don't care how pretty he is." We both got a good laugh from that one.

"At any rate, little girl, when we gonna blow this pop stand? I hope you didn't eat but one of those damn hoagies because I do have a good meal prepared."

"Bro! I've been thinking about which one of my favorites you were going to be cooking up all day, but you know I ate the Pringlaye hoagies. That lady knows my heart."

"I forget who I'm talking to. You are the only woman I know who eats like a hog and still holds it down."

"Just shut up, called me a damn hog, and now I'm sexy. Wow!"

While dashing to the door with the ease of two teenagers horse playing around, he turned in my direction and said, "You know Ms. Piggy was my favorite Muppet, right?"

We got back to the main hallway just in time to see the last family leave. Mr. Niles had started his cleaning. A weird man but a terribly great worker. He volunteered for the job and refused to allow me to pay him. He works for Big Slim back at the Schuster Hill Funeral Parlor. The support I get from this community really knocks me right off my feet daily. I stood there, glimmering on my reality, and looking at how simply blessed I am.

The staff and I got in our circle and did our corny high-five to the success of another session and went our separate ways. When I got to my house, you know who was already there and in the kitchen. The presence of fine Chinese cuisine slapped me at the door.

"You do know this is called breaking and entering, right?"

"It's not breaking and entering when I have a key to the balcony door."

"Jayden, who the hell does that? Wait a minute. I don't have a balcony." Jayden grew up in this house with his favorite uncle and knew how to come in through the basement.

"I've been meaning to get that basement lock changed."

"Don't you remember I did that for you like a year ago? You gave me a key to the front door because you were locking your keys in the house so often. Girl, you need to empty that filing cabinet of yours. DECOMPRESS DECOMPRESS! It can't hold all that shit you trying to stuff in it. Just ain't enough room."

Dinner was exquisite. If I didn't already know, it definitely confirmed why people come from across the country to stop in at his restaurant. There's a reason why he can afford to charge prices close to forty-five bucks per meal. When you think of healthy Chinese food, you expect sacrifice in quality and definitely taste, but you have none of that with Jayden. We sat in the living room, discussing life, and entertaining each other with the experiences of our day. Then he took on his serious face.

"Lucy, my family used to be servants and slaves in this very community. My dad's side was owned by the Millwright Family, the Millwright Marijuana Dispensary now sits on what used to be the old slave plantation. Mom's side of the family was tricked over here by the Great American Lie of a land of milk and honey and untold riches. When they got us over here, we had to work as servants a little bit higher than the black slaves but nonetheless slaves. I'd be lying if I told you there wasn't sometimes a hidden disgust lurking within me towards whites. Over the years, I wanted nothing to do with this place. Every time I tried to get away, I had my mom to think about. I could never convince her to want to leave, and I surely wasn't going to leave her here alone. It took me a while to change and learn to turn my lemons into the best damn lemonade on the continent. Truth be told, it was Pringlaye that would stop by the store every day with one of her engaging stories on humility. The love and concern she showed towards Mom and me really changed my perspective. Believe it or not, we were close to shutting down about five years ago. As the family advanced off the plantation like most Chinese, we setup grocery stores to serve the blacks and the whites separately. My Uncle Raymond who owned this very house, had his store on the west side of town with the whites, and we were here behind the tracks on the southside with the blacks. Both stores knew disparity. The whites would take their strong-armed advantage, and the blacks were just barely able to feed themselves. At any rate, when Mom took ill with the big C, I had to come up with a way to afford her the best cancer treatments and get us off the poverty line. Growing up, I was always surrounded by good food and great cooks: Uncle Raymond, Mom, Grandma Lucy, and Big Slim were the best. But neither ever wanted to do it for a living. They didn't think that people would support them. Mom had to take an extended stay at the cancer center for about six months, and the 25 percent that the insurance left for us to pay quickly depleted her life savings. Lucy, over her lifetime at that point she had saved a measly 100k, and four months into her stay, 75 of it had cooked away to doctor bills. Ms. Pringlaye started stopping by the store daily, catching me crying, and every day she'd say, "Puddin, your moma gonna be fine, and so are you. Now lock the door and cook yourself out this slump.

"For a few weeks, she'd come over with a sandwich in hand and that same saying. Then finally I had that eureka moment, she wasn't talking about eating to get my health up. Every day that I wouldn't follow her command, people would stop by the store, asking if we served meals. One evening I sat up in the house crying and snotting all over the place. I had been praying to God for a miracle, and I heard Pringlaye's voice ring in my head, 'Puddin, your momma gonna be fine, cook yourself out this slump.' Man, it was like somebody else took control of my body. I went to writing out meals for the week, went to our herb garden and collected everything I needed. I called my five broke cousins to the shop and started cooking a lunch menu, and we haven't seen a broke or slow day since. God gave me a favor in every sense of the term, and when I heard about your foundation, I knew it was my time to give back. I talked to Pringlaye, and she got Mr. Richmond onboard. People come from across the country to eat a meal from our shops, and I know it's all because of God. He says, only what you do for Him will last."

I sat there with tears streaming down my face, just taken over by his testimony. I never would have imagined how he got to this point in his life. Who knew?

"Dude, that's amazing. I thought all of y'all were selling drugs and had a giving conscience working in my favor." We laughed hard at the thought.

"Lucy, girl, you kra kra." But again, with a serious look in my direction, he added, "Said you had something serious to talk about; let's hear it, my dear."

He sat there, all eyes and no words gazing into my soul. He looked on me as if he could see what I was slow to speak about, yet he sat patiently waiting to hear me. I sat there, preparing the words of my soul to lay it all out on the table.

"Lucy, I'm here for you always, better or worse, good times and in sorrow, and I expect nothing more than what we presently share. Now be assured you can trust me. Why am I here?"

Reaching in my purse for the gold foiled envelope, I said, "Jay, I need you to tell me what you know about this." I saw the very fear of God reflect from his face like that of a clear mirror.

"A flame waiting to burn. Where'd you get it from?"

"So, I have been told. Yesterday, Raychelle and Sadie almost had a breakdown just from seeing it. What am I dealing with here? I need to know, and you're the only person I can trust to tell me."

"There are these invisible strong arms that run this City. Children suffer from the misfortunes of their parents. The children are abducted like the little Ramirez boy and never seen again. I don't know what they do with the children, but their disappearance is usually linked to the

28

dealings of their parents, something to do with a blood contract. If it seems like the parents are going to renege on the deal, they usually turn up dead from something reasonable like an allergic reaction or a car accident. The only clue of their presence is that damn envelope you have in your hand. That's all I know about it, baby girl. Don't ever ask any of these town folks anything about it. Like I say, we don't know who is involved. This has been going on in town for a long time. The players have yet to be flushed out. I remember hearing my granny speak of the founding families for Schuster's Landing, the Wright's, the Lloyd's, and the white Schuster's (you met the black Schuster's up there at the funeral home with Big Slim and Ms. Ellis, that's an interesting tale for another night). But these people called themselves saviors. This community is about 150 years old, and those same families are calling the shots here in town under new names from marriages, but nonetheless, the same wolves are snatching your sheep. All in all, this isn't something to play with. You got a son and your own life to consider."

"Jayden, I'm always considering us, but where does the circle break? These people are destroying lives, and everyone is too terrified to do something about it. I won't live in fear. I got to do the right thing here."

"Lucy, there are worse things than fear to consider here…the unknown is worse than death. But like I said earlier, I'm willing to go the distance with you. But we gotta be smart about this thing. I don't want either of us to wake up dead. Let us work on this in secret. But there is one person we can trust and depend on for knowledge, that's Big Slim up there at the funeral parlor. But listen, I gotta get to sleep because that shop not gonna run itself for lunch tomorrow."

I sat there a bit freaked out about what he had told me. It was then that it dawned to me how spooky this big six-bedroom house could be. Go figure, a 30-year-old woman scared to be alone in her own home.

"Jayden, it's late, why not just stay here tonight." Those comforting words just rolled from my tongue sounding so soft and sincere, knowing all along it was only serving my fear of being in this big ass house all alone tonight, but it really was too late for him to travel around this city at night. We don't need another black man shot by the police; besides, Jayden lives above his shop, and his mom is still in the hospital.

He immediately started laughing at my request. "Let me find out, big bad Lucy-Lou is scared of her own self shadow," he said as he fell out laughing.

"You can laugh your ass off today and tomorrow, but don't leave me here alone tonight. You have just scared the absolute hell out of me. Come on, Remi's bed will suit your short self, just perfect."

"With all that wine we've drunk tonight, I don't need to be driving, and the last thing I need is an accident or get pulled over by that no good ass Chief Marcelle. You know he's a legend, right?"

"Because of his police career?"

"No. No. Hell Nawl! His dad signed the contract, and mysteriously died of a heart attack. Everybody knew of his dad's struggle with every addiction known to man. Marcelle's mom sent him to live at the Schuster Orphanage claiming to be unable to provide for him, but rumor has it she got a gold foiled envelope too. But here's the catch, they gave her an option and longtail short he ended up becoming the Chief of Police after old Rodger Beasley clumped over. He trained him personally for the job, though. But enough wives' tales for tonight, let me go get my gear out the car."

"You came prepared, huh?"

"Baby girl, I'm a single man with plenty of oats to sow. I gotta have my gear ready for you young dazzles in distress. Be right back, my little dazzle you."

I woke up this morning to a funk floating all around my mind. I kid you not, it felt like the world crashing down on my head. Sometimes I'm a victim of giving up. I have such significant momentum at times and then it just disappears. I just don't understand... I shared my bedroom with one of the most beautiful caring men in town. Any other woman would be trying to jump his bones, but no, not me, I have to be responsible. I can't do what my body so desperately desires. I think If I didn't have Remi, I'd say goodbye world and walk off a cliff somewhere. Why did I have to be the statistic? I do all these great works, and I can't even get laid without thinking about this condition that has taken refuge in my life. My doctor told me my numbers looked great. She also said if she didn't know better, she'd say I was cured. Go live a healthy life Ms. Lucy. They say. But how in the hell can I do so with this monkey on my back? My mental well-being could and probably should be a subject of discussion. I have yet to comprehend the toll that this condition has taken on my mind.

For the most part, I wrap myself up so tightly in my child, the foundation, and loving my friends that I hardly ever have these moments of deep despair, but when it does get a moment to rear its massive head, it falls on me like a million-pound weight. I want to be in love so badly, I was never meant to be alone. This shouldn't be my prison. So, I sat there on the floor of my closet, looking through the old family album. Crying silently, desperately needing a hug from my mom and dad.

It's 4:45 a.m., my normal prayer time. Moments like this always remind me of Dad. He used to tell me whenever you wake up from sleep, it's time for you to go ahead and start your day. That theory has stuck with me over the years. Despite rising before the chickens, I still claim to be a night owl. A little prayer couldn't hurt right now. Just as I started to pray, I could hear a familiar sound, almost like piano music. Actually, the song is more familiar than the noise is strange. I just now heard this tune at the funeral, but who the hell is downstairs playing it? I sat there, frozen in my seat on the floor wondering. God, somebody is in the house, what am I to do? It hit me that Jayden is less than ten feet away from me on the outside of this closet door. So, I tiptoed across the floor and peeped out the closet door to hopefully get his attention, but he wasn't in bed anymore. Now I really had the chill!. Where in the hell is Jayden? Have they gotten in the house, snatched the man and are now waiting for me? Now I can smell bacon and pancakes.

When it became apparent that Jayden was downstairs cooking breakfast and playing the piano, I felt like a fool. A man of many surprises. He'd never said he was a musician. His playing was so similar to Ellis and her mother, Aria. I must have really traveled far in my thoughts and became void. His knock on the closet door startled me with a scream. He snatched the door open like he was ready to bust open a can of whoop-ass.

"Lucy, what's wrong?" he exclaimed as he jumped in the closet like the caramel ninja.

"Oh nothing, you just startled me is all," I responded with a nervous laugh.

I then added, "Didn't know you could play the piano."

"Oh yeah, my Aunt Ellis and my granny taught me when was about five years old."

"Ellis and Big Slim, are you family?"

"Didn't I tell you last night that they were my folks on my dad's side?"

"Dude, you said a whole hell of a lot last night, but I don't remember this bit of information. Talk about a small world."

"Yeah, come on out, I prepared breakfast. Sorry about the noise. I always loved playing that piano. It belonged to my Aunt Audrey; they never played it and didn't allow anyone else to touch it. Uncle Raymond would let me tickle the ivories when she was not home."

"It is a beautiful piece of history. I always wanted to learn to play but never got around to doing so. Maybe you could give Remi some pointers."

"For sure. Now come on downstairs before everything gets cold. I gotta get going home. Did you have a good sleep? You were sleeping well until you started screaming and fighting. Do you remember what that nightmare was all about?"

I sat there, ate my pancakes, and pretended like I didn't remember. When, in fact, the dream is so recurrent that I can go scene by scene and not miss a beat. I wished that it was just that a dream and not a real-life nightmare. I wished I didn't have to live be reminded of the residue of my yesterday. Sometimes I would sit and look at Remi and wonder to myself how such a beautiful child came from such a horrifying moment. I lick my wounds and count my blessings every day when I see that my child is healthy and doing fine. I shuddered thinking about the moment when he'll start inquiring about who his dad is…how am I going to tell my baby I don't know? What will he think of me when he knows the truth? Even worse, what do I think of me?

"Baby girl, where are you right now? I should be the one zoning out and shit, after all, I was up half the night waiting to shield you from the boogeyman. What's on your mind? Come on, talk to me."

"Jayden, I can't do this."

"Can't do what?"

"I can't keep my promise to Mrs. Ramirez. I was really scared last night. I can't be in fear and raise my child at the same time. I can't be watching over my shoulder constantly for some mysterious unknown force to appear and hurt me. And it's messing me up on the inside. I got to let this go. I want so much to figure it out, but I can't put us all in danger chasing behind yesterday's ghost."

"Lucy, you don't have to do anything you don't want to do. I mean, I understand where you are coming from, but like I told you last night, I'm your ride or die, whatever way you want to go. If I have to stay here with you every night, I'll do it. You can depend on me. And don't be tripping too hard on that Ramirez woman, she didn't give it all to you. I hate that for Raphael and even her, but you're not God. You can't fix it all. You do a great job with the kids you're influencing at the foundation, and without you, there would be no opportunity like it for those kids. You are making a difference, my dear. This thing is going to work out sooner rather than later. Just keep your head up."

"Thanks, man, I needed to hear that. I really was feeling worthless. Thanks for everything, keep cooking like this and I might just take you up on moving in with us. Remi would be thrilled."

"You know I'll do it for you. Just give me the word. But listen. Are you good?"

"Yes."

"Okay, well, I'mma get going. If I remember correctly, today is our day to prepare the meals for the kiddos."

Following him to the door, we stopped and embraced like a real couple. He squeezed me tightly and whispered in my ear, "Keep it loose but keep it tight, baby girl." I stood at the door and watched as he drove out of the driveway.

Something deep within felt assured that all would be well. I didn't have to be at the center until 1:00, so that freed up some time.

It has been a few weeks since the first disappearance. Somehow I've managed to keep my head down and my mouth shut. But nonetheless, I've been working nights in my basement stringing this spiderweb together bit by bit. So far, I only have the abducted children and their parents on the board -- no real links to the original families. The only interesting key piece of information is that on the night of each disappearance, the Police Chief never showed up to the crime scene. Conveniently, there has been something as equally wrong happening in town during the time of the events. Every child has been a participant of the foundation. The children mostly all come from two-parent homes. The fathers have left the wives to deal with the aftermath of it all. And get this, the families affected so far have all been Spanish with the mothers totally out in the blue when it comes to details of what might have happened. The age of the children ranges from 10 – 14 years old. Months before the disappearances, the families have been known to struggle financially. Something changes their faith, we now understand this comes up to be the signing of the blood contract. Each wife but Mrs. Ramirez had a chance to enjoy their husband's sudden windfall. From my understanding, Dave, her husband, ended up getting too drunk at the Electric Cowboy and beat a man to a pulp and ended up on the run.

No one knows if he's dead or alive. His family has ceased to exist, and he's on the run somewhere or buried under the earth. But the others climbed up the ladder and then were snatched from the high mountain to the ground. I imagine when it really sinks in that you've sold the future of your child to the unknown, the men have to either end it all or slip away from their shame. Either way, it's death to the family, then the children disappear, and the gold foiled envelopes appear. It's somewhat reasonable and so easy to just want to believe that the kids are running away from their terrible living conditions to an even worse fate beyond the border. Their lives have appeared so small and replaceable that people like me saw their absence, yet we didn't understand what lived right under our noses.

With my newfound knowledge of each disappearance, my heart seemed to chip away. The dreams of Mrs. Ramirez have become more and more recurrent. In each dream we always land at our final scene in the police station where instead of her being terrified to be taken to the hospital she walks away calmly with her back to me voicing, "You said you would help." I usually wake up drenched in sweat scrambling out of bed. Jayden checks in with me two to three times a day and we meet up at the range to work on my shooting skills. Considering the situation, we both agreed it was time that I learn to use my gun. For my 16th birthday my father's brother Uncle Jack, a retired special ops military man gifted me a Glock that the parents were not too happy to see me receive. I never got trained for it. But at any rate, between Big Slim and Jayden, I've made some real progress. The majority of my practice has been with Big Slim. The woman stands about six feet tall has brown copper skin, with shoulder-length solid white well-kept dreadlocks. When she's not overseeing a funeral she can be seen in a combination of blue jean skirts and a nice pair of sneakers. She always looks casket fancy. The things that are happening in Schuster's Landing shine brightly in my face like a mirror when I'm around her. I do my best to conceal myself and just blend in with everyone else. Like with Jayden, I'm comfortable enough to talk with Big Slim as she likes to be called. I know I can trust her. We talk a bit about everything each time I see her. I thoroughly enjoy hearing the stories of her past and how her family came about owning the 25-mile stretch of Schuster Hill Township. She was going on about something in her deep rustic voice and I must have zoned out because I didn't hear her calling my name till she grabbed my shoulders and started swiftly shaking me to and fro.

"Lucy-Child, you can't do those children no good if you lose yourself." Thinking she was speaking of the foundation, I brushed the message off.

"Big Slim, the kids are in great hands with my staff. They make the foundation what it is today with very small guidance from my hands."

"Lucy Child, you know full well I'm not talking about that foundation. But while you are mentioning it, you might want to take silent inventory of your workers, keep an eye out for your Judas because they there taking note of you." My ears were taken back by this revelation, but in my mind I certainly could believe it. After all, Jayden did say there are a lot of invisible players to this game.

"Stick with me, child. Here in a little bit the light to your path will connect all the dots. But as I was saying, you got a Judas keeping tab on you but Imma be your Ananias for a while. Last weekend when I was, taking old Bessie for a ride I saw that child Raychelle out there on Old County 8 getting out of ole ugly Marcello's police truck. Now that's a man to keep three eyes on. Your two and the good Lord's One. All this gonna come out in the wash, Lucy, don't' get confused by the rinse cycle."

"Big Slim, I don't rightly know how to function past this thing. They are worrying me in my dreams and every day I'm reminded that I didn't keep my word with Mrs. Ramirez."

"Lucy, that woman done ran her race and unfortunately somebody cut it short, but it was her race to run. And she's not truly worrying you. That's your conscience pulling on the strings of your mind trying to get you to forgive yourself. See, guilt got a way of making things appear wrong. What you promised that woman was nothing more than the human side of you trying to appease another upset soul. You are going to keep your word, no doubt about it, but we gonna do it the smart way, baby. Now get off your ass and cock that rifle, there's a war coming your way and you needs to be ready. Fire!"

Indeed, it's funny how things change without notice. Here I thought I had one of the most loyal teams in the world. But things got strange around the foundation. The dots were finally starting to connect. This crew has been here since the inception of the foundation. In fact, Raychelle and Sadie were originally staff members of the now-closed Shipper John's Elementary. Here I was thinking all this time that I strategically placed teams over programs that they are both knowledgeable and comfortable performing. All the while I was setting families up for failure. These women head the parent enrichment program. That's like placing a zebra in a lion's den. They are able to gain an investigative perspective of the parents and like any normal human being, the parents unload their lives to these two thinking they really have a confidant. All the while the wheels of wickedness are churning along like a well-greased machine. The parent enrichment program usually consists of a very successful financial boot camp course. There is no need to pry when everything is laid out on the table in this class. My insides cringe at the very fact that we have innocent people here seeking to learn how to become free of debt and manage their means efficiently and these snakes are devouring their innocence. They don't teach the classes, we're in collaboration with the local bank who sources two instructors each fall and spring session. They innocently help the participants to gather their credit reports and make a note of the truly distressed parents. I don't know the specifics of this journey but I'm sure like Big Slim said it'll come out in the wash and today is the start of the wash cycle…program success audits. My theory needs to be tested.

I made it into the office around 8:00 a.m., and deactivated the alarm long enough to get inside the building and into the main office. I needed the participant listings for the last two years of the financial boot camp workshops. Like any good criminal, I fully expect the cocky bastards to have left the evidence in plain sight. After all, you can't find something you never knew to look for. The files were indeed in their rightful spot. As I reviewed the list alongside the city's missing children list, I literally saw the dots. Besides the names of the six missing children there stood a pronounced red dot beside their name on our roster files. The last dot was on Raphael Luis Ramirez, the sixth missing baby. His name was the only one that I truly recognized, and I know that's because during the beginning stages of the foundation I was only supervising and focusing on the administrative duties with Reggie.

I sat there silently crying as if there was someone else in the building that would question my tears. I dropped this ball, no other way to view this thing. I didn't really notice any of the parent names but it was mostly married couples that came for the class. We usually see a great deal of the mothers and not the fathers because they are usually the laborers of the family. However, in this case I was guessing the wives were able to persuade their husbands to participate. With the women not working and having any debt themselves, it would indeed be the men who needed this class the most. It was just a theory until I saw the spring session 2001 participant listing read **Helen and Hector Ramirez,** parents of the missing Raphael Ramirez. No further test needed for this theory now turned a sad fact. These wretched people have had this thing down to a science.

With all this new revelation, I know there must be a link I'm overlooking. So, I reviewed the participation list over closer. We do a great job here but I don't care how free and wonderful the programs are…in order to get the mommas and papas to participate there's got to be some type of worthwhile incentive. Moms will show up but dads need persuasion to come. It was like the clues were dropping from the universe, waiting for me to open my eyes and start looking. The program executive summary listed program incentives for all participants. If they attended each of the five Thursday night classes they would receive a certificate for a loan with Landing Bank. While reading this information, I can't even begin to explain how I was feeling. The rage in my heart was unbearable, just to think these people entrusted the lives of their families with me and I failed them. My spirit wants to taste blood on its teeth. I glanced down at my watch the alarm had started to buzz. I'd set an alarm for 30 minutes before 10 a.m., as I didn't want to raise any suspicion amongst the group. Strike like a king cobra.

Reggie would soon be coming in, so I needed to get the area cleared and get out of the building. I didn't want his catty self to drop any nuggets of my presence to anyone. I need to keep the routine as regular as possible and can't go spooking the wolves. I need his head and can't get it making noise. I quickly rammed the copies into my bag and exited the building to find Chief Marcelle conveniently passing through. I saw that black Tahoe turning onto the street just as I flipped the locked gear. So much for being the pink panther, but I'm still in charge of this situation. I casually continued on to my car, not once glancing in the direction of the approaching vehicle. By the rate of his slow cruising, something told me the joker wanted to play a game of friendly chit chat. As I threw my bag in the car, he approached and rolled down the passenger window.

"Good morning, Ms. Sanchez"

"Greetings, Chief Marcelle, to what do we on this side of the tracks owe this visit?" I asked smiling ever so fondly.

"Ms. Sanchez, do you consider yourself to be pretty observant? I mean, you must, to imply that I never patrol in this area."

"Indeed, I am just that and I implied nothing; I spoke fact. I've never seen so much of you until Raphael went missing. However, I meant nothing by the statement. In fact, I'm glad to see you doing more of your job."

"I guess I'll take a compliment anyway I can get it from you, Ms. Sanchez. Know that I take my job seriously. It's intriguing to know your eyes are open. Enjoy your day, Ms. Sanchez, bask in its beauty."

"We just gotta keep breathing, Chief Marcelle."

He smiled and started to pull off.

"Hey!" The truck stopped and I walked forward five paces to again look in the window at the good Chief. "I never got a chance to tell you thanks for all your efforts with the Ramirez case. I know I might have come off strong, but given the situation I'm sure you understood, but nonetheless please accept my apology. I have a son and I can't imagine him running away. I forget that children can sometimes be more troubled than we adults. Have there been any leads on his whereabouts?"

He sat there and looked delighted and in awe of my charm. Then he said, "You know, here in this area I deal with children running away a great deal. Like you said, we can't imagine the pressure and abuse these kids have and are enduring daily. When you walk around appearing invisible and live in silence like they do, you can't see the options. With us being so close to the border, we have reasons to believe they escape to an even worse life in Mexico where I have no jurisdiction and have to give up the fight unfortunately. In the case of the Ramirez kid, I believe he ran away to be with his father. You know he was undocumented and was deported back to his country. The kid probably couldn't take being fatherless. His mom's death was just an unfortunate coincidence."

I nodded in agreement with the bullshit he was spewing. Knowing all along this kid didn't just run away to Mexico. What kid would want to go to that life? We catch plenty enough hell here in America.

44

"And thank you, Ms. Sanchez, it's refreshing to know that someone other than myself knows that we are doing our best when it comes to this job. If ever you need anything, here, take my card, my cell is on the back. Call me day or night. I truly respect your presence here in our community. My son has thoroughly enjoyed the foundation and looks to be coming out of his shell. Have a good one, Ms. Sanchez."

His smile appeared sincere, but I know the difference.

My ways are not like your ways and my thoughts are not of your thoughts.

People are always discussing how woke they are, but no one ever said how tiring the wokeness can be or how it adds so greatly to your paranoia. My day went well despite wanting to slit the throats of the two women. Due to other circumstances, we had our weekly staff round table meeting on a Tuesday rather than on the usual Monday.

On the surface everything appeared to have functioned as usual. Reggie was on his cell pretending to be giving me his undivided attention, then came his hysterical uncontained laugh and the "hey, let me call you back, we're in a meeting." That joker can't whisper for shit.

"I was informed today by the school district that the timing of its standardized testing this term, instead of it being held in the late spring session, it will be the two weeks before Thanksgiving break. Our curriculum goals will have to be adapted to accommodate the change, guys. Unfortunately, our resources for the parent enrichment programs will have to be reallocated and actually postponed if not canceled this session."

Sadie and Raychelle spoke in unison. "Will this affect the whole parent enrichment program?"

I knew they would love this answer. "Guys, to tell you the truth nothing is set in stone just yet, but the board wishes to tentatively postpone all programs that aren't directly required. To accommodate this change we are going to need all hands on deck. We do know that the college-ready and GED programs aren't optional, the bylaws require their presence and we can definitely continue to accommodate those services. However, the financial boot camp workshop will be put on hold until we see different."

I sat there at the head of the table looking flustered by the call at hand but ever so intently watching the reactions of those in attendance. I knew that the two cousins would likely show some sentiment of more frustration than the other staff members. After all, it was their plan's bread and butter facing the ax. Everyone else sat comfortably with the decision. Sadie sat there biting her nails and Raychelle looked as if someone had taken her blankie. I sat there quiet for a reason and shook my head in a means of disgust, again keeping the full details from my staff. Then I stood to my feet to replace a file in the cabinet behind my chair. I slammed the drawer shut with a WHAM and regained my seat.

"Guys, I'm sorry but this just pisses me off. That Superintendent had all summer to provide this information and now a month into the session we get the memo. We're all supposed to be together in this thing. This moment tells the true story. I've also found out that the school district is working on its own similar program with hopes to force us out by the next school term. It seems like the wolves are attempting to come down out of the high country for a good sport. But be that as it may, we're going to continue making the difference."

I needed my words and moves to be meticulously calculated but at the same time appear to come from a frustration led by the seat of my pants. Something tells me Raychelle is the force and little Sadie is just our well-meaning friend but nonetheless a deadly enemy because she's a follower.

"Well, guys, I can't think of anything else, the floor is open to you all. But one more thing, I'm going to need someone to stop by the school and get a printout of the test coverage for all grade levels that will be testing, but other than that, have you all anything that needs our attention?"

The room remained church house quiet except for Reggie again pretending to not be on the phone. "Reggie!"

He nearly jumped out of his skin and dropped his phone.

"Well, we have our instructions and I know I'm always saying this but thank you for your service. There would be no 'Sharp Minds Bright Futures' without you and the children of course. I need to run a few errands and I'll see everyone this afternoon. Reggie, who is providing the meals today?"

"Ummm, let me go check, Ms. Lucy, you working me hard already this a.m.!"

Everyone exited the room with the leading ladies at the back of the line looking a bit thrown.

"Hey, Sadie and Raychelle, I'm sorry about cutting the program. I know how hard you two work to make each session a success. I was thinking maybe we can still have the program after the testing season has concluded during the month of December, think about it and let me know what you think."

They nodded like twins and continued to exit the room, still looking frustrated that this had put a dent in their plans, but it had limited my direction as well. But this might be a better distraction than previously thought. Only time will show.

"Hey, Reggie, I need you to sign this." Since the session began, I'd had it in mind to correct a wrong that had gone on a bit too long. I handed him something I'd prepared a year ago but kept putting off in hopes that he would do better. You can't let a sore fester too long or it'll start to smell. I handed him his first formal write up. I had no intent to fire him but I needed two things from him: the fear of termination and renewed dedication. He looked upon it and immediately went to pleading.

"Ms. Lucy, I'mma do better, please forgive me."

"That's all I need to hear, Reggie. I love what you do here for the foundation, BUT I need you to be more responsible. I believe what you're saying and I'm holding you accountable to do better. Now I need you to check in with Ms. Pringlaye and make sure there will be no problem with the meals and pick them up. I have some errands to run and I'll see you later. Sign this, place a copy in your personnel file and leave a copy on my desk. When we know better, we do it."

I exited the building feeling good about myself. Raychelle was outside smoking and talking on her phone. She ended the call no sooner than the first sight of me. I didn't hear anything but I suspected she was speaking with the Chief. I walked past her and got in my car. The wretched bag of bones looked rattled -- but nothing like I plan for her to be.

I stood there in my closet trying to decide what I would wear. Every time I come in this closet I say the same thing, we need to clean this thing out! It makes no sense for this one woman to have so much. I happened to glance over at my phone to get a handle of my time. I noticed I had three voicemails from Reggie. When I saw his name I smiled and decided to only check one voicemail, and no doubt as I was expecting he was calling to provide updates on all the things I had requested and more.

"Ms. Lucy, sorry to disturb you, I just wanted to make you aware that I took care of everything you requested. And I picked up the mail from the PO Box and stopped by City Hall to find out what you would need to submit that USDA community facilities grant. Thank you so much for this opportunity. I promise no more slacking, Ms. Lucy, I'm going to do everything I can to redeem my character with you."

In listening to the message I was delighted in his response to the write-up. He took full responsibility for his actions and I imagine we won't have any more problems from here on out. He is a great worker I just needed to press a bit more greatness out of him. And then there was the doorbell. I wasn't even going to go check the door until my phone started ringing...it was Jayden.

"Girl, come open this door."

"I'm upstairs, use your key."

"I already did, just needed to make sure I had your permission to come in."

"Dude, what the hell? I'm in my closet, come save me."

"Hey Hey, dude, what's up? What you doing do this way?" He stormed over to the loveseat and tried to look like a mad puppy dog.

"That old hippety hop preaching bastard finally got to me, Lucy."

"Jay, I know you didn't let the good Reverend get under your skin did ya? Back in May that ole crane told me I was gonna forever be an outsider in this community. After I turned down his advance to taste my bubble gum as he called it."

"That sounds just like that wannabe do-gooder. Reggie didn't call you?"

"Yeah, he called but I didn't talk to him. Come on, tell me what's up?"

"Well, I was down at City Hall to pay my water bill and the Good Reverend was already in there chatting about nothing with that rude nosy City Clerk Ms. Holy Ghost Speak in dead tongues Sirleene Ingraham. The water clerk Ms. Humbreye hadn't yet returned back from her lunch, Sirleene fills in when she feels like it. If I were Humbreye I'd go on lunch and never come back. So, not wanting to cause any mess I just came in and took a seat and decided to be patient. Then came Reggie. By the way, what's up with him, he was super not his usual catty self. The boy was rocking the hell of that Professional roll. At any rate we sat there talking and waiting and Reggie started telling me about Ms. Janie Stewart's homegoing celebration over the weekend that went on too long because the preacher decided to pray, sing, preach and start all over again. And that humped back bastard stopped talking and said 'you can't blame the pastor for doing his job. From the look of you, his work was in vain'. Reggie didn't say a word. He's gay why can't they get over it and leave the dude alone? Then the old bastard said 'you still a faggot ain't ya, boy?' Then Ms. Sirleene no good ass started jumping and shouting JESUS JESUS! Preach! Pastor, God don't want no homos at His table."

"Wow, see, that's why I use that dropbox. That woman will make you want to drag her behind a boat through a lake of glass. But I'm on a higher calling these days."

"Yeah right, MS Higher Calling. You know you're monstrous. I told both of them off. Her damn husband has been caught I can't even count how many times giving and receiving mustache blowjobs out in the park. I said, 'I got one I got one...hey, why don't you go home and work on that gag reflex and just maybe your husband will give Alderman Geoffrey's jaws a break.' She burst into tears and when I looked the preacher's way, he must have thought I was finna whoop that ass. The man turned, started to run and fell right through the glass door then scrabbled around in the glass, got up and took flight to his truck running like an old

51

camel. It was so bananas, that I didn't even see the Mayor. He walked out the back all red-faced from laughing and apologized for the city clerk. He told her to go get herself together and be in his office in 20 minutes. I hope he's gonna fire her no good ass but of course she's an elected official. Every year these voters put mess in these offices and then they wonder why it all falls to hell. He told me to not worry about the water bill and took Reggie to his office. Now between me, you and the gatekeeper you know that Reggie been getting that man's money for a long time on the low-low. But I ain't mad, at him, sometimes you gotta do you."

I laughed so hard that my eyes had started to tear up and my cheeks were sore. I wish I had been there to witness it all.

"But, Jayden, sounds like you got justice, what the hell are you so mad about? The Mayor covered your bill. Sounds like everything went in your favor."

"I'm mad about not taking my chance to whoop that old man's ass. You know I've been replaying this scene in my head. I saw myself pick that crane up and throwing his ass through that window onto Main street. The ghost must have told him to tear ass preacher tear ass because I was ready to handle business today. I'll get my chance one day, he never learns. But at any rate I got to get back to the restaurant, my crazy ass cousins will be in there busting jokes and forgetting all about the customers. Go ahead and get lost in that cave you call a closet. I think I can let myself back out."

I stood there still laughing to myself at his antics and had really forgotten what I was supposed to be doing. Then it hit me, Big Slim overheard me humming while she was making the organ sing at the parlor a few days back and told me my voice was beautiful and that my natural key is Ab. I got invited to sing a solo at the funeral of a dear friend of hers. She said it would be to my benefit to get noticed at this funeral. There would be some people there that my future would be well pleased to call a friend. I hadn't sung in the public since I was in college but the breathing techniques stayed with me. Big Slim told me to find something jazzy to sing and don't worry about her because as she so confidently said, "I can give you a run for your money, homie." I got dressed and began mentally shuffling through music but couldn't come up with anything. It would be apparent I didn't even try to come up with anything if I hit the ever tired but faithful "Amazing Grace," furthermore no one wants to hear that at a funeral. That song in my opinion is just like that freaking "Order My Steps." I like the song but I absolutely hate to come to a funeral and hear it sung. It's like no one notices that hey somebody is already dead, why slay their loved ones with the saddest death tone song. I'm like Aretha, give the folks something they can feel like, "Jesus Brought the Sunshine."

Whenever I sing I think about my, mom that woman could blow. She liked to sing old down South gospel despite being born and raised in Los Angeles. She and Dad ran a nightclub when I was a teenager and on Sunday nights choirs from across the community and neighboring communities would be there for the gospel showcase. She would often open the show with 'Save a Seat for Me' and my dad would accompany her on the organ and the house would be on fire all evening. I mean one act after another had a part in tearing the kingdom down. Big Slim asked for a bluesy number and I figured it couldn't get any better than 'Change is Gonna Come.'

The funeral parlor can accommodate three funerals concurrently if needed and the parlor rooms are named after the directors (De'Ellis, De'Aria and De'Jon). The De'Aria room is used predominantly for funerals with the others rented by small churches that don't want or can't afford to build a sanctuary. Little Julian greeted me at the door with an obituary and triplets ushered me into the choir stand. Ellis was leading the choir with the "Lord is Blessing Me." The family while being seated was swaying from side to side with the music. I have to forever say these folks really know how to celebrate a life. I took my seat in the back of the choir chiming in with the background and glancing over the obit and was surprised to see this service was for Miss Shirleen Pride, the nice colorful old lady from the library. When I first moved into this community she stopped by my home with a chocolate pound cake that my taste buds still haven't gotten over. She was only 65 years young. I'll bet it was the big C, if the heart attack and stroke don't get you the Cancer doesn't mind being Johnny on the spot. In looking up I was shocked to see the City Clerk beaming my way with a welcoming smile. If I didn't know her mask I'd believe she was a sweet delightful woman and would probably sympathize with her being walked on and over by her husband but evil is as evil does.

In looking over the landscape of the funeral I was amazed at the colorful attendees of her funeral. There were reps from all levels of state government here. Her obituary read Miss Pride worked in the state capital for over 30 years as Deputy Governor and was adamant that her small communities weren't lost in the shuffle. Her most prized accomplishment is the Schuster Landing Indoor Water Park Resort on the outskirts of town. It competes with being one of the largest indoor water resorts in this part of the nation and second on the top three list in the country. It's not too often that you get a chance to hear countless people speak on someone's good works at a funeral and their words be true. This woman's life stood for something that surpassed her existence. Her life was nothing short of a legacy that people around the world should aspire to emulate.

Then came my time to sing. I knew Big Slim told me she wanted me to do the solo but I was shocked to read Sis. Lucy Sanchez listed as the soloist. I walked up to the mic up front near Big Slim and did as she instructed and started to sing, and when I hit that 'I was born' note she made that organ clap like thunder and from there I don't know what got into me but I doubt I'll sing ever so well again. Who receives two standing ovations at a funeral for Christ Sake?

The funeral went better than well and at the repast I was greeted by so many who knew of my great works in the community with the foundation. Senator Charles English gave me his card and told me to give him a call next week as Ms. Pride had been working with him to get the foundation designated as a community learning center. The funding from such designation would really open doors for the foundation to do even greater works within the community and for our youth and their parents. I couldn't believe my ears. Senator English told me, "If I die tomorrow I want your voice to ring my bell to heaven."

I left the parlor stepping on 10 feet tall stilettos damn near touching the clouds. Before I got fully over the door I heard my name.

"Lucy Child!" I turned in her direction to see her holding two thumbs up and a smile the size of the Hoover Dam. Big Slim turned and went back into the meeting room. I have had some great feelings in my life but today was unlike anything I've ever before experienced.

It's amazing how strange things can get when you mix up a lot of betrayal from a familiar place. For years my motto has been to move around and mostly get out the line of fire, but not this time; I fully intend to be that perfect mixture of gasoline and diesel this situation needs in order to burn. The journey back to the foundation was a moment of true surrealness. I entered the facility from the back entrance which is usually reserved for emergencies, but something told me fighting through a myriad keys was worth the effort today. In looking at the time, we had approximately 30 minutes before the magic would begin. I wasn't expecting my smoking gun today but let's say I believe in miracles. I made it to the midpoint of the facility which we are awaiting funding to convert into a public library and computer lab and really no one has a reason to walk this wing except to dream of its tomorrow. Only I wasn't the dreamer today. I heard voices. I threw myself into the old broom closet and closed the door all but fully just to leave a small crack for air and my ears. It was as if someone was coaching my investigating spirit but I didn't need my phone to alert anyone of my presence. Amazing it is how we can be led to the right place at the right time. In listening I recognized the voices of both Raychelle and Sadie, then chimed in my trusty assistant Reggie.

"Ladies, what are we going to do about this bitch? You can't tell me she's not on to something. Ralph says there's nothing to worry about but I know better. I've dealt with people like her before and they don't give up easily, she's worse than a hungry black crow. She's not gonna leave this be."

Sadie stumbled and bumbled around her words and then said, "Y'all, Ms. Lucy is the least of our concerns. She doesn't know anything, she just a fool hell-bent on helping the world be a bright light."

"Right, Sadie, after your big blowout scene the other day and my explanation that bitch was scared almost shitless.

You should have seen her eyes when I told her about our cousin."

"What cousin? What happened?"

"Boy, you remember Cousin Margie died from the sickle cell may her soul rest in peace. But I told her that the order abducted her and how it just fucked Sadie up. She does have one of the gold foil envelopes from the Ramirez kid. Thanks to you, Reggie! To think I explained our game to her yet she'll never unravel it to the core."

I thought to myself that she missed her calling in Hollywood. They traded laughs back and forth about my stupidity. Then the laughs came to a halt with Reggie posing the million-dollar question.

"Again I ask, what are we going to do about her? We can't let her get in our way."

"We're not going to do anything to her. Marcelle is keeping an eye on her. He intends on getting in her head and seeing what's under those Brazilian bundles. In the meantime, keep everything the same, don't change a thing. What we do need to do is figure out how we can get that boot camp class back up and running. That damn Superintendent needs a private visit."

"Well I don't know about you ladies but I got to straighten things up and walk right. I got a write-up this morning. I thought I had gotten fired this morning. I had to get my shit together quick. I wasn't expecting that from her. We have to be ready for her. I don't care what nobody says, she will strike like a cobra and we gotta stay three steps ahead of her. Ralph says there is a midnight meeting at the old mill tonight. The gatekeepers will be present bearing gifts. So clear your schedules, it's going to be a long rewarding night. Our hard work finally gets a payoff. It's time to make these donuts, ladies, let's go attempt to save these kids from the anguish of their stupidity."

"10-4!" they chimed in unison with laughter.

I stood there in the closet for about five minutes clenching my phone almost in disbelief of what I just heard. What happened to these people? How did they get so comfortable with being evil? Where the hell is this old mill? So many unanswered questions. I creeped out of the closet slowly hoping not to be seen but I needed to get back to my car before they could see and suspect me. When I saw the coast was clear I took off down the hallway like death was on my trail. I needed to get to my crew. I know Big Slim and Jayden will know the way to this old mill. I left the parking lot nearly hyperventilating. My heart pumped harder than a small water pump trying to clear Big Muddy. It's both enlightening and unsettling to again learn that the very people I have trusted for so long are nothing more than monsters. I would have never guessed Reggie was in on this too. I kept hearing Jayden's words "you don't know the players of this game" repeating like a broken record in my mind. Immediately I knew I needed a reason to be absent.

"Bright Light Foundation, how can I be of assistance?"

"Reggie, it's Lucy, tell Raychelle and Mr. Theodore I need them to fill in for me today. A pipe gave out on my water heater and my kitchen is trying to go down like the Titanic."

"Oh my gosh, do you need some help? Mr. Reilly is a Mr. Fix-it."

"Oh no-no-no. I need all hands on deck at the foundation. Besides, I'm a WOMAN, Reggie, there ain't no project too big or too small for Miss Lucy. I got this, Sir."

58

I abhor lying but today it's worth the effort. I'm with it all. Figuratively speaking I wasn't really lying. The excitement of today had my stomach breeding a pool of butterflies, it felt like at any minute now the bottom would drop. I barreled the car into the driveway and bolted out of it like a bullet behind its prey. I sat there on the toilet in the midst of my stomach convulsing back and forth with my thoughts going in a million different directions; everything led back to this mysterious old mill. I've lived here for almost three years and I have not once heard anyone mention an old sawmill. When the war in my stomach finally ended I glanced at the time and decided not to call Jayden after all. I knew chances were slim to none that Big Slim would not be entertaining the death angels with a funeral. The phone rang about six times before she answered.

"Lucy Child, what you got, girl!" She always answered the phone like she was anticipating a fire.

"Big Slim, where is this old Mill mine? They got a meeting tonight and I got to be there."

"Mill mine. Mill mine you say? It's one up the ridge from the estate, ain't been nobody up there since I was a young woman. My daddy and uncles worked there for years. Now who you say having a meeting up there? Hell, if they knew like I know they wouldn't be playing around up there. Place subject to detonate anytime."

"If one was going there would they have to come by your place?"

"Only way the public can get in or out. "

"What do you mean the public? Is there another route?"

"Yes, through the old family cemetery about two miles behind the parlor cemetery. We haven't used it since my ma died but that's where us Schuster's all used to be buried, even the others till they got too uppity."

"Okay, me and Jayden will be there by 9:30. I'll explain everything when I get there. Bring firepower, and Mister Niles." The call ended.

Before I could hang up good, there was a banging at the door. The way they were knocking I would have sworn it was Marcelle but of course it was Jayden. Reggie just had to call somebody to come to my rescue. Just like a man to ignore my wishes, but talk about front door service, my soulmate knew to come see me. Must have felt it in his bones. I swung the door open to him carrying a tool bag almost bigger than him.

"Did it trip the breaker before the water started spewing everywhere, Lucy? " He talked but never stopped walking till he was in the kitchen closet no doubt expecting waist-high water. He opened the pantry door, looked up down and all around and started scratching his head.

"Hey, Lucy Lou, come here for a minute." I smiled and moved in closer.

"Um, Lucy, where the hell is all this water Reggie's old dense ass was telling me you were over here drowning from when I went by the foundation to drop those meals off for the workers?"

"Wait, it's not your day, what happened to Mr. BBQ Richmond? He asked you to fill in for him or something?"

"No no, I saw Reggie when he picked that up earlier. I made some special meals for the workers trying out some new recipes. I had a plate for you but I left it when I heard about this false alarm. Now what the hell you got going on, girl?"

"Bro, come sit, come sit. You won't believe your ears."

After explaining how things unfolded I decided I needed to get to the office. After all, this would have been the first time that I would have ever missed a day. Despite the dark situation, I'm not interested in allowing these assholes to ruin my stellar attendance record. I returned to the foundation to find everything running smoothly. To an outsider and even the old me would have made the grave error of mistaking these folks for solid, good staff members. So glad I now know better. Before long Reggie was on my heels kissing up inquiring into my water heater fiasco.

"Ms. Lucy, were you able to get that water heater problem taken care of?"

Still with my back facing him I smiled and wheeled around to greet the face of this lowlife. "Oh yes, Reggie, I was able to get everything all squared away. Turns out the thing might have been just as old as the house. It was time for it to finally play out, I guess. I'm just grateful that I was home when the shit hit the fan. Those hardwood floors and carpet would have been ruined for sure."

He stood there pretending to be mesmerized by my every word. I wondered if the no-good bastard had a conscience, but likely not considering his present job outside of the foundation. Seeing as I was doing all the talking I started to turn and get going only to be stopped again.

"Ms. Lucy, I really want to tell you that I'm sorry you had to write me up. I'm really fortunate to have this job."

I gently smiled and looked him right straight in the eyes and said, "Reggie, I have always greatly appreciated your very presence here over the last three years. I used to hope I would never have to find out what life without you here would be like."

He stood there smiling while I was speaking but towards the midrange point his smile appeared troubled.

"Ms. Lucy, are you firing me?"

Looking equally as surprised and confused as him I nervously laughed.

"Reggie, no….Um, no, sir. I was just saying I have this assurance you'll be here for years to come, hopefully as my assistant director. You are the best, Reggie. You stood up to your shortcomings and without hesitation stepped up to being the man I knew always was hiding within you. I'm too pleased to have you here with us. Just keep up the good work."

By that time his Bluetooth headset began flashing red and blue. I conveniently excused myself and continued down the hallway to the tutoring area to look in on Raychelle and Sadie. Upon entering the room I was soon approached by the ladies. They both hoped all was well with my water heater. I simply smiled and said, "Ladies, all is well, all is well." With that I exited the room.

The anticipation of today's possible revealing of players had started to eat away at my insides. I had to go give myself a quiet coming to Jesus moment to calm the hell down. There were so many factors at play in my mind. Just the sheer idea of finally gaining some sort of perspective on the people behind all this mess had my gears grinding. I don't think I've ever walked the halls as much as tonight. I kept passing the fire emergency signal for a moment the 16-year-old me started to consider pulling the switch. The present-day me was so close to pulling the tab when Mr. Lyles aka Mister Wierdazz began tapping my shoulder. His touch was like that of lightning bolts shocking my unsuspecting soul. If he had been my killer I was dead at this moment. I wheeled around to his voice with my eyes about the size of golf balls.

"Oh, Mr. Lyles, yes yes, what can I do for you?"

The slender built, tall husky-voiced man stepped in close and whispered, "Wanted to know if you didn't mind if I did the rest of the cleaning first thing in the morning. Big Slim needs me at the parlor around 9:30."

"Oh, yes sir, no problem. Have a good evening, Mr. Lyles. See you in a little bit."

He nodded his head and disappeared back down the hallway. A true man of few words, I could definitely see him taking someone out like in a horror movie and then continuing his job as if he didn't just massacre half the room. Nonetheless, I felt we might need his qualities tonight. Who knows what might pop off tonight. I got some attendance reports that need to be forwarded to the education department. With my nerves being on the fritz I tried to go occupy my thoughts with something of substance.

Finally, the last child and parent were out the door and the crew was all signed out and outpouring into the parking lot to their various cars. I spotted the others loading into Reggie's black-op edition Grand Cherokee. Given the night is still young they are likely headed to the Silver Dollar, their usual bar. Sadie raves on about their mojitos and hot wings. Part of me wanted to follow them around all night but I knew that wasn't a smart move. Every time I got ready to go against the grain and play private eye I heard my dad's husky voice "be anxious for nothing, Marie." It's amazing how the voice of reasoning within us can channel up old sayings and thoughts that were considered to be long forgotten. My dad's been gone nearly 15 years and my thoughts of him can sometimes come in fresher than yesterday. In respect of my dad and the correct way to handle this situation I lingered around the foundation checking the doors and lights. Usually, Mr. Lyles is still around making his trot from room to room but of course it's all on me and honestly, I feel a bit strange. There's an eerie feeling going down my spine that's getting stronger as I get closer to the back entrance. I almost feel like I'm not alone and that there is someone watching me. I had one earplug blaring slow jams but this feeling made me stop the music and start to be cautious of my surroundings. I kept looking over my shoulder every so often and by the time I got to the last classroom on the left I stepped into the room and shut the door. I shuffled through my phone for the surveillance app. Making the foundation light up like a Christmas tree and channeled in the surveillance cameras. As I viewed each area for this crazed killer being I saw something that made my heart start pounding like a bass drum. Panic was all around in my being, what was I going to do? I can't call the police. My thoughts were so loud in my head that I just knew anyone in the building could hear them. I stood there panning the camera views for other intruders but didn't see anyone other than this one figure. The person was just standing near the door no doubt waiting on me to come back down the hallway so they could pounce on me like a cat. I twisted the doorknob again making sure it was secured and stepped away from the door. Looking around for the perfect lethal weapon, right now would have been a perfect time for my gun. It was in the car. It does no good to have a concealed carry license and a gun and not carry the thing around with me. Then I looked at the camera number and up at the number above the room door: it read Twenty-three. I was my own self silent killer that was tracing all around the room waiting to strike. I'll be damned! My own self shadow freaked me the hell out for just almost 35 damn minutes. I couldn't believe me I looked at my phone and said "speak of this never." Lordy, how in the hell am I going to be comfortable tracing about a dark forest tonight when I'm running around preparing to kill myself. I must have hit something but somehow I made the recorded footage for the day replay and I could see and hear the children singing. It hit me that I could replay the scene from earlier with the others.

I had the cameras installed before the foundation started considering all the incidents with children occurring. The guy did tell me the audio of the cameras would likely one day outweigh the cost of the system. I remembered agreeing with him but thinking "dude is just lying and taking my money." My smart workers knew about the cameras but never considered what looked us all in the face each time we had to replay footage...at the bottom of the 42-inch screen were the words in lime green...MUTED. Even though I knew I was alone I streaked back up the hallway like a track runner. I got to the front entrance saw that no cars remained but my own. At this moment their whereabouts served my interest. I just needed to get in my car and up Schuster Hill to the parlor and the new Highway 65 was my path tonight.

Traffic through downtown was horrendous because of that Asia-Ja Boy Concert at the 'REP'. The constant stopping and going bore gifts tonight. In glancing to my right I spotted Reggie's car paralleled parked and three cars ahead was the black Tahoe with the spotlight on the left mirror merging into traffic with its blue and red lights flashing. Only I didn't spot the other players nor their cars.

The Tahoe made a swift U-turn right in the midst of nearly gridlock traffic. The pissed-off onset drivers flashed their high beams and dug into their horns rather deeply. With the charades of the moment I saw a quick flash of the silhouettes of the three in the back seat of the big tank of a car. At least I assumed it was them; could have been anybody actually.

I need to get to the parlor but at the same time going just didn't sit in my spirit. I kept attempting to just drive home but on the flip side I needed to be on my way to the parlor. I pulled to the side of the road three times, almost as if I was an involuntary participant in a strange game of tug of war. I fought traffic to get back on the road only to snatch back into a mysteriously available parking spot. My first mind and the second-guessing had gotten the best of me. I literally didn't know what to do but sit there in the car and look crazy. I managed to pop a U-turn on the crazed street with the convenient luck of doing it right in front of one of Schuster Landing's finest. I'm going down tonight for sure. I sat there like a deer in headlights still wrestling with my conscience. All-day I could not wait to get to the parlor, then when it's time I can't calm my mind enough to make the drive. Mom always said in moments like this just follow the right decision and it'll prove out later. Still I sat there waiting on the officer to tear me a new one, while fidgeting with the right thing to do. I was so caught up in my thoughts that I never saw the officer get out of his car no less approach my car. He tapped on the window and I damn near left my skin. In rolling down the window I nervously smiled hoping to not appear suspicious

"Good evening, Officer. I'm so sorry."

"Ms. Lucy, is there a fire?" Looking even more confused as to how he knows me. My mind was scanning through familiar faces like a hawk but I was not placing this man and it must have been showing

"Ms. Lucy, I'm Officer Eugene Ruston, Harley's dad. Don't tell me you done forgot me already."

"Oh my God, Mister Eugene, I'm so sorry. I just couldn't piece your name and face together. I'll be the first to say it's been a long day and soon to be an even longer night."

"Longer Night?" Now here I am over talking myself! If I could just think straight I could be on my way.

"Got some student evaluations to get laid to rest before tomorrow's deadline. I know I don't have to tell you about paperwork and deadlines."

"Yes, yes, ma'am, excuse my tongue, but I know all about that shit. I was working on a report when you just decided to pop a U-turn on South Main Street. Only a woman on a mission would dare even try such with these silly Soul-Ja Boy fans scattering like ants. But listen, don't worry about nothing, just be safe and remember this."

"And what's that, sir?"

"Be anxious for nothing, what's for you is for you. You don't have to run it down, if it's for you it'll cross mountains and high hell waters to get to you. Have a good night, ma'am and I'll tell Harley I saw you tonight."

"Thanks, Eugene. You be safe as well."

A voice of reasoning will travel through many different channels to get to its students. I sat there and waited until Eugene pulled off. It dawned on me that I never once said a thing about his little one. The man must think I don't care. Leaning my head on the steering wheel I kept thinking what the hell is up tonight? We've got somewhere to be and why do I need to go home? I could see from the dash clock it was only about 8:15, plenty of time for me to get home to my destiny and then get up the road to Big Slim's place. Just as I made my mind up to go home I could hear the sirens and saw a line of blue and red lights from a distance coming my way going in the direction of the New Highway 65, then the alert on my phone started blaring. Something tells me I dodged a bullet. Sure enough when I checked the message notification it read: "15 car collision on northbound Highway 65, six injured and two fatalities, updates will be provided momentarily. Traffic is redirected to Old County 8."

I couldn't help but think that could have been me, my guardian angel put in some work to save my life this evening. I'd been so wrapped up in my world that I never looked to my right to notice I had planted my car right in front of Jayden's shop. He stood ever so patiently there on the sidewalk waiting for me to come inside. Again, my phone was buzzing with another news update. The body count just went up to 12. I smiled and proceeded to open my door and in the blinking of the eye the door was torn off the car and sitting on the road about 20 feet ahead of the car. Sitting there numb, I kept thinking death really is but one step away. My son could have been parentless.

I sat there trance-like watching the people tracing all around the car screaming my name.   My name was almost called at the great roll calling. Jayden kept holding my hand and asking if I was okay. Yes, I was a bit rattled. But the urgency to get to the parlor all of a sudden was rooted deep in my mind. We have somewhere to be and it seems the universe is trying its best to throw a wrench at us. I overheard someone say that the police were on their way but it'll be a while considering the pile up on the highway. Jayden asked for what seemed to be the 100th time, "Lucy, are you good?"

I was confident I had answered him each and every time. Looking him square in the eye I asked, "Jayden, what the hell is wrong with you? You've asked me the same thing over a hundred times. Yes, I'm good but we really need to get going."

"You haven't said a word since your door was thrown down the street by that damn black Escalade. Can you believe they kept going? A damn drunk driver has no love for no one. But that's alright, I'm sure my camera got that tag number. But, dude, get your purse and let's go in the shop."

"I really haven't said anything? I thought I had been answering you for the longest."

"No. Nothing, just been sitting there clutching the steering wheel and looking at the time on the dash like you were calling your time of death."

"Well that explains why you weren't answering me. Man, I just keep thinking about I could have been gone."

"Yeah, I'm glad you're okay though. We gotta be more careful. That freaking drunk driver was all in the parking right of way. I can't wait until we get that young tool identified. Do you need anything to drink or eat?"

"Just some pink lemonade. Do you think we can get going to Big Slim's, its' almost nine. I can go to the station and make that statement tomorrow. Hell, the status of my baby will be the same tomorrow."

"Cool cool. I parked in the back, we'll have to go through the kitchen. Let's go."

Out of all the time I have spent here in the shop I've never ventured a tour through the kitchen or the back living quarters. We disappeared through the office back entrance down a hallway with two doors, one to the left and one to the right. The left was chosen, it entered the room with the stainless steel chromed appliances with the fellas doing what they loved. As usual my name was ringing all over the kitchen. The fellas were busy speaking in English and laughing in Chinese. Only they and the Creator knew what they were saying. Before long Jayden turned and yelled something in Chinese in a harsh tone and all laughs ended. I'm sure they were teasing him considering how red his face had gotten.

We were soon ripping down the street in his cherry apple red Audi. I secretly envied his taste in vehicles. He seemed to be muttering something down low to himself. I couldn't make out any of it.

"Jayden, what were the guys saying?"

"Singing a damn Lucy and Jayden sitting in the tree lullaby? Those bastards get on my damn nerves sometimes."

"Dude, calm down. They're just having fun with you. It's apparent we're just friends."

"That's just the thing, Lucy, I don't want to just be your damn friend. I want you. I want all of you. I knew it from the first time I met you. And about 20 minutes ago I could have lost you before our love could even begin."

He started to choke up a bit when he said the last part. I kept my eyes straightforward really not knowing what to say. I knew he had feelings for me. Hell, even I for him but I can't put him at risk.

"Jay, I'm sorry I can't give you what you want, It just isn't fair nor safe. I do love you and even more than any friend but…"

"But what, Lucy? I'm not worried about these invisible gangsters. What's so hectic about your life that you can't allow us to get lost in each other? I want to spend my nights lost in your thoughts and wake up every morning to your beautiful voice singing over the shower. And you know I adore little Remi. Really, I've been trying to control this but after what happened tonight I just can't hold it in anymore. Lucy, I want you and I know you want me too. So what's the deal, let me know something."

"Jayden, I have HIV and I don't know who Remi's father is because I was gang-raped in college and the damn name isn't really Lucy it's a nickname. Well legally it is now but I was born Marie Antoinette Martinez not wanting to remember the shame of my past. This also reduced the risk of being discovered by the people who murdered my parents. I became Lucy Sanchez over 10 years ago. You're right, we are perfect for each other but I can't and I refuse to put you at risk. I'm sorry I never found the right time to share this with you. Don't hate me. I ran away from my past and have nightmares every night that forces me to look back."

The tears flowed from both our eyes. Not knowing what he would think or even do. He surprised me when he wrapped my hand in his.

"Lucy, we can get through and past that, I've been taking PREP for years. I used to be the neighborhood hoe. I'm blessed to not have AIDS or worse, be dead. And I'm sorry all that stuff happened to you my dear. When this is all over tonight I want us to give us a try. Okay?"

"Okay. I'm willing. But promise me this, whatever happens I don't ever want our friendship to end. You are the best thing since my Remi."

"Forever Friends, my dear, and don't worry about nothing. All will be well."

I don't know how he did it but we pulled into Schuster Hill at exactly 9:30 passing the parlor to park in the garage at the grand ole house. As the garage door was rolling down Big Slim opened the side door to the big house dressed in combat wear. He looked in my direction, smiled and said, "Well, war is hell."

The doorway led to the kitchen of the grand old home. I could hear the little ones upstairs laughing and having fun amongst themselves. There stood Ellis glaring in our direction with a look of pure disgust; she looked pissed. When she saw Jayden, her facial expression became even graver. She just stood there and said nothing. I wondered what her deal was but then there was no need for the wondering when I knew for myself that her fear of the unknown was maddening. We followed her around past the kitchen and into the sunroom off from the living room, where we found Lyles already planted on the plush Queen-Anne sofa dressed in dark combat attire like Big Slim. On the coffee table before the sofa were five sets of what appeared to be night vision gargles, handguns, and backpacks filled with other war items I suspected. I took my seat, wondering exactly what the hell I had really signed on to do. Big Slim quickly disappeared and promptly returned with two camouflage jumpsuits in hand.

"Here, you children go get changed. I don't know where the hell y'all thought you were going in them getups you wearing. But no worries, Big Slim gonna get you straight before long."

Without question we stepped into the jumpsuits and quickly regained our seats.

"Now listen up, on that table are some night vision goggles and silenced handguns and on the floor are backpacks with some supplies. I don't expect any trouble tonight but we gonna be ready if shit gets strange. We going down there just to get the lay of the land. There is no room for senseless mistakes. These folks have been hiding around in my territory for this long with no one living willing to trade their existence for the truth. I want to get in there and I want us all to get back home safely. Do you hear me?"

Everyone nodded in agreement.

"Now we need to get going. One other thing, leave your cell phones here, they won't work in the mines and the pitch of even the smallest notification will travel around. We don't want them to know we're there. We just need a good handle of what we are up against. Now come, let us get going. Ellis, stop your worrying and trust your momma, child."

"Momma, you don't always have to be the damn hero. You always take in the stray circumstances. This is city shit, let the city folks handle it. Lord knows we don't need any more attention. That damn man is taxing us enough."

"Ellis, hush that up. You know better than any other just how tangled we are in this mess. You're right, we don't have to be but we ought to want to do the right thing just because it's right. I can't have these folks one day deciding they ought to leave one of those blasted envelopes here in place of one of them children upstairs. God said don't worry. My job is to trust. Now we'll see you sometime likely after midnight, go get some rest and I'll see you in the morning.

"You just get back safely, I'll be waiting right here. If you're not back before the darkest part of the night I'll know what to do."

With a grave look of nervousness, she closed the basement door behind us. Big Slim ushered us down into the basement with Lyles leading the way to the back door with the Old Schuster Cemetery in sight. When she closed the door, she said, "Lord, here we come" and took her place at the head of the line again speaking, "Children, come on in here. We got a journey to walk."

The moon hung brightly in the sky shining almost brighter than the sun. We walked through and past the cemetery with the moonlight shining so brightly. I was able to read each of the old tombstones we passed. After about 35 Schuster family members we came to the forest, upon which even the bright moon didn't dare shine. Everyone pulled on

75

their goggles with Lyles and Big Slim leading the way. We might have walked about 25 minutes through the forest and were nearly out when I considered the dangers of the forest such as the snakes and possible foxes and wolves. Surprisingly, the only life form we encountered was a hoot owl that in mid-step Big Slim turned and shot off its post above us. I knew she was a good shooter but damn, who kills an owl for doing his job?

"He won't hoot another soul away from here."

We were 30 minutes into our forest hike when the moon's glare could be witnessed yet again and ahead stood the mine's three entrances. The leaders went straight for the one in the middle with Jay and me following suit. Again, the night vision goggles were direly needed. If I thought the forest was dark, it compared nothing to the mines. Stopping midway of the entrance, Lyles removed a rope from his bag and tacked a section of it to the wood wall support post and regained his post as the leader. The journey continued down the shallow shaft until two gunshots ricocheted throughout the mine like explosions. Though it echoed loud and close, Big Slim waved us to continue forward. I'm guessing her judgment of the distance knew better. It wasn't long before we got to the origin of the sound and there laid stretched out on the floor my smoking guns all dead except Reggie, who whimpered like a scared pup choking on his blood silently begging, "Please PLEASE!"

The deal was sealed. We stood there amazed in the darkness with no words and no way of revealing the shooter. The fruits of our labor provided small strokes of failure. It all appeared to be in vain. It had been exactly two weeks since we all saw what we saw in that old mine shaft. Running the office has been a real struggle without them. Even though they were terrible fucking human beings, they actually did their jobs well. Jayden and I have been taking turns staying at each other's homes. Everyone has been doing their best to stay on the low but resume our normal routine. The truth is the shooter could be any number of people. I have no proof that the three were really riding with Chief Marcelle. What I saw could be purely coincidental. In my mind's eye I know I saw them in that car hours before their deaths. Chief Marcelle is indeed connected.

It'd been a while, but moments of that night still haunt my mind. We all escaped into the shadows of the dark just as quiet but even quicker than we came. By the time we made it out the mine shaft and hit the dark woods again the thought of a wild animal was far from my thoughts. Big Slim is about 80 or 83 years old and that ole girl was leading the pack like a true alpha. She ran that trail better than her younger counterparts. We chased behind her like the very pits of hell were on our heels. At last, when we were at eyesight of the basement door Jayden tripped over his twice great uncle Jimmy Dean's tombstone. Crashing to the ground whew chile he fell hard. At the sound of wood creaking, Big Slim stopped dead in her tracks and yelled FREEZE. Everyone halted like soldiers in the army.

"You're sitting right over that old cistern, don't even breathe too hard. Lucy Girl, how far are you from his hand? Can you reach him from where you stand?"

"I think I can."

"Don't do no thinking, child, save his ass or them out there won't be the last dead you see tonight."

I thought my heart had seen the worst of this night. I looked down to make sure I was on solid ground and none of that old wood. Jayden extended his hand. I reached with the strength of my ancestors and snatched the nearly crippled man to safety.

"Damn, Lucy, you snatched and slung my ass around like a rag doll." We all nervously laughed with much consideration of what could have been his demise.

"I have meant to get that thing properly covered."

"Jesus, I was almost gone, y'all, don't need that damn thing anymore. I'm coming over first thing tomorrow and get this shit taken care of, Grandma."

"Don't worry yourself none, child, I'll take care of it. Let's get in the house."

"Nawl Big Slim I got it!"

We sat there on the basement floor in the dark. I don't know what anyone else was thinking of but I had kept looking back to that mine floor at Reggie whimpering for mercy. After a spell Big Slim began to speak.

"Somebody got tired of that bunch and they fixed the leak. By God, Lucy, somebody done blew you for your hop and took your king. It goes without saying but tonight didn't happen. We done sho'nuff hit a wall but we not boxed in. But until we regain sight of the trumpets it's best to tip light. I don't know about y'all but this ole lady here is tired. This here house got plenty of room for everybody to rest comfortably through the night. There's some whiskey in the library closet to help with ya nerves if need be."

By the time she finished speaking, Ellis had appeared in the midst of the darkness and almost made me and Jayden break camp. Our eyes had adjusted to the dark and with the faint luminance of the moon breaking through the window I saw Big Slim smile at our skittish nerves.

"Oh, I could have told y'all Ellis was in the room. This child gone get the hell knocked out of her yet. She has been easing up on people for almost 40 years. Thank Lyles for teaching her such madness as a child."

Her charm could make a goliath smile and rethink his ways. When the laughter and mind warming conversations were made, and everyone had retired to their rooms, I lay there in bed in pitch darkness still trying to make sense of it all. Sleeping was the furthest thing from my mind. Stringing this thing together was my main objective. The drink I sipped on before bed was supposed to make me mellow out and relax but it was like an energy drink. My mind went even further in the pits of nowhere just that much more. I could not believe those reprobates were really dead. Just to stand there in the dark listening to Reggie's voice bubble in a pool of his own blood just kept troubling me. It's a damn shame this isn't a Friday night. At least I could have the weekend to try recouping but in less than three hours I have to get to the foundation.

Now there's a thought that made me sit up in bed. Locks, security codes and all that has to be changed. Whoever the hell murdered them could be prowling through the foundation right now. It's not secure. I wanted to call my locksmith Darryl at that very moment. As rational as the thought seemed to me, I knew it was irrational as all get out. So, I lay there looking at my phone and waiting to see the first peek of sunlight.

The hours seemed to have stood still. When you need time to roll it does quite the opposite. After about 20 to 25 glances at my phone I decided to not look at it anymore and sat there thinking it was probably 3:00 a.m., the usual darkest moment of the night. The witching hour. Just as I was about to glance at my phone again my alarm went off and woke me up, it was exactly 5:59 a.m. I don't know when I dozed off to sleep but if you'd ask me I thought I was awake all night. As I sat there on the side of the bed no doubt looking crazy there was a light knock at the door. That threw me for a loop. I had one of those moments where I knew where I was but at the same time I thought I was in my own home. When all of this has settled, I'm going to seek some much-needed couch therapy.

"Lucy, are you awake, it's Ellis?"

"Yes, ma'am"

"Do you mind if I come in?"

"Yes yes, please come in "

I couldn't remember where the light switch was, so I just turned on my cell's flashlight. She hit the switch as she came into the room. Laughing at the sight of me with a flashlight in the daytime.

"Girl, put that flashlight down, you acting like one of them woman that's strung out behind one of them old no good fellas."

Only someone of our generation would know anything about that old song. She took a seat beside me on the bed and positioned herself to look me right square in the face. She's definitely her mother's daughter. When I talk to her on the phone I always find myself looking in attention as if she's beside me looking in my face.

"Momma told me about what happened down there. This Schuster Community does one of a few things to you when it comes right down to it. You keep your head down and do your best to pretend like you don't see the world crashing all around you until one day it's no longer an act. Or you get reckless and put yourself and anybody connected to you at risk. Or you learn to maneuver past the smoke of this present time's bullshit and make headway towards better by putting this place in your rearview mirror. Now you're a strong woman considering what you've been through, that little girl you left out West ain't you no more. Hell, you don't even wear her name. So, I don't expect you to put your head down and for damn sure ain't looking for you to get scared.

80

Scared people turn into dead people. I got my family here and you're now part of that family. We gone sift this shit through and through till it's a fine flour. Do you understand me ? "

I wasn't feeling strong but the strength and courage I saw glowing from her hazel textured eyes gave my strength life and my soul told my mouth, gal, I dare you to say anything but yes. Try me why don't you.

"It's good that we see eye to eye on this thing because I didn't want to have to play Harriet and put the shotgun on your back. But rest assured I would have. Now we got breakfast ready downstairs and Cousin Darryl is on his way here to see what needs to be done about securing your foundation."

"How did you know? "

"You don't do what we do and not know what to do, baby girl. I set some towels and a toothbrush in that chair over there for you and there's a bathroom down the hall to the right. We'll see you downstairs in a bit."

She exited the room and left me in wonder. What the hell do they do?

Sitting around the breakfast table with everyone truly felt like family. Fond memories of my childhood and my parents surfaced tears of joy in my eyes. Jayden being himself gently squeezed my hand and whispered in my direction.

"This could be us. Stop your worrying, everything is going to be better than alright, just you wait and see. "

Deep within I wanted to believe that but somewhere crouching in the darkness was the truth and it knew things were so far from being alright. I ate about four of the flakiest pancakes covered in a chocolate jam when I remembered I'd missed my meds last night. Its no biggie so long as I get them taken before 9am. Everyone's stomach was tighter than dick's hatband. Knowing the task at hand Mr. Darryl started to excuse himself and beckoned for my attention in the hall.

"Ms. Lucy, you don't have to worry about a thing. I got everything I need, all I need from you is a new security pin. Give me that and you have nothing further to be concerned with. I can let myself into the building if you give me your key. I should be done by the time you get to the office at nine."

"Thanks so much, Mr. Darryl. You're a number one lifesaver."

"No worries, child, that's what I'm here for."

It is so comforting to know that I don't have to fight this fight alone. After bidding everyone a see ya later we ventured home using the new highway as old County 8 would have made us give up those tasty pancakes as a toll. The ride home was quiet, obviously there was much to discuss but it felt right to just enjoy the moment until I spotted that damn black Tahoe sitting to the side of the road. Immediately my heart began to race and my hands trembled. It was like he was waiting just for us. As we passed the Tahoe the lights began flashing. The creeper smelt my fear. Jayden must have been still caught up in the moment because he continued down the highway paying no attention to the siren blaring or the blue lights flashing.

"Jayden Jayden! Pullover, he's behind us."

"Awe damn. Stay calm, he doesn't know anything. We were just coming back from a date in Greenville. Let me do the talking."

The car pulled to the side of the road, our exit to the house Exit 9 Fair Park Blvd was in sight and less than a mile away. He whipped out of the truck like a shot rabbit and stood outside the window with his ugliness brimming over.

"License and Registration."

Leaning down into the window he glared around the car and stopped at the sight of me.

"You two in a hurry? Got yourselves a deadline to meet?"

"No, sir, just kinda lost track of the speed. Sorry about that."

"Pretty Boy, you were going 75 in a 55 zone and you mean to tell me you just lost track of the speed, huh? Lucky for you my ass is loaded with paperwork from that train accident last night. I'm feeling a bit liberated this morning. So I'mma save my shots for later. But let me catch you again, Pretty Boy and I'll nail your ass to the cross. Have a good day, love birds."

We sat there until he drove off. My nerves were on the fritz and Jayden was fuming. He knew just what to say to make his insides boil over.

"I can't wait until we deep fry that son of a bitch. And I don't give a damn who he has on his side."

"See, he must know something. We've got to be careful."

Jayden didn't respond but I knew he agreed. We were soon getting ready to pass the shop when I decided I would go ahead and get my car from the back instead of waiting to have him pick me up later. After all, I needed to keep appearances and some normalcy in my life and continue to be seen around town.

"You sure I can't drive you home and have one of the guys bring your car by the house here in a little bit?"

"No, I'm good, Jayden, if this is gonna work I have to be a woman and not be a scared little girl. I'll drop by later. I actually have a lot to do today before the day begins for the children."

"Well you know to call me if you need anything. Don't hesitate. I'm coming by the house tonight when the foundation closes with dinner so keep your taste buds ready."

"Thanks, bro. I don't know what I did to deserve your friendship."

"Just being you my love, no more and certainly no less."

When I finally got to the shop it all clicked. There sat my baby with plastic taped over the spot where her door should have been. On first sighting laughter poured out of us. Don't ask because I can't explain it.

"Guess you gonna be needing that ride after all little lady."

"Um, kind Sir, can I get a ride home?"

"I'll get my boy Marcus to tow it to his shop until your insurance can determine what to do with it for you. I sure hope my camera caught that tag number. I wouldn't be surprised not one bit if that Marcelle didn't have something to do with all of this mess. He probably hoped to knock your ass off with those other psychos. But the police better get they asses in gear and get a report made for you. Pronto! Or I'mma start shooting my damn shots."

"Calm down, dude. I'm alive and well that's all that matters. We could have been like them. But somewhere somebody was praying for our keep."

When I finally made it to the office, Mr. Darryl was just about done testing the system and double-checking entrances for any oversights.

"Hey, Ms. Lucy. I got you all set, here are six master keys. If you need anything further or more copies give me a call. I went ahead and upgraded your surveillance system storage as well. You can now easily download specific days from your computer. Where the system used to overwrite every three months, I added enough storage so now it overwrites only every nine months."

"It backs up to the cloud before overwriting, right?"

"Yes, ma'am, it does. Do you remember how to gather those uploads? If not, I can show you right now. The system has gotten so much more user friendly since last year's upgrade."

"Darryl, I don't think I have ever really known much about this cloud feature and Reggie usually handled the technical stuff."

At that moment it became apparent that even Reggie didn't know as much as I thought he knew about the system. If he had known about the audio recording feature he would have used better discretion. But then again he could have been on my side and hoped to come clean one day. Only God and death knows now.

Darryl and I went through the specifics then he left me to it. I stood there looking around realizing that it's all on me for now. Indeed, I have a lot to overcome but nothing is more important than securing this building like Fort Knox. Sitting at the conference table I tried wracking my brain to write out everything that needed to be done. I must admit I'm sorta lost without Reggie being here. I don't know how I'm going to make it through today. Before joining my reality I have to play the game of calling their phones. Like always I don't know who's watching and not watching. I don't know the players of this game but deep within I know the play depends on my move. I shuffled through Reggie's desk in hopes of gaining an understanding of his work. To my gain, his agenda binder outlined things well enough for me to know where to go. I hadn't performed in this capacity in almost two years. To simply say I'm lost is a gross understatement. Cross-training rotations will definitely be in place during the next hiring season. A few minutes into it, everything started to click and make sense again. I hope his soul rests in peace.

After getting the bill invoicing knocked out of the way the natural prowler in me started searching through his desk. I don't know what I expected to find but finding three busted cell phones wasn't high on the list. This wasn't a significant find because it's a general consensus dude is lethal to phones. But when I went to open the bottom left drawer my attempt was fouled by the lock. It was no match for this woman and her mission or her trusty drill. The thrill of what I would find made me nervously anxious. When I got the drawer opened and saw it only contained the old petty cash lockbox the suspense died. I could have just screamed. I thought we'd trashed that thing after it stopped locking. He must have been somewhat of a hoarder. Determined to discover if his desk had some Rosetta stone clue, I searched the back walls of its compartments but came up with nothing. Then when I picked up the lockbox it was heavier than I remembered; not expecting anything special, I thought he must have been using it to store candy bars. The boy loved candy. Indeed, it was storing the best kind of eye candy….greenbacks perfectly wrapped, and rubber-banded to a thickly packed manila envelope. That envelope was my interest's smoking gun. Just as I was about to ravish its contents my cell phone started ringing. It wasn't a number that I recognized, so I ignored the first two times it called but some persistent Annie on the other end was relentless because they called back a third time. I answered.

"Hello, Ms. Lucy, this is Officer Eugene with the Schuster Landing Police Department."

Thinking he was calling with news on my car, I interrupted, saying, "Oh yes, good morning, Eugene. Randy's Towing Service is taking the car to his place over on Roosevelt Road."

"Ma'am, I was calling to report that your employees Reggie, Raychelle and Sadie were a part of that pile-up last night and sadly they didn't survive." I had forgotten to even make an attempt to call their phones. You know, for good faith.

"Pile up? Wow, they were a part of that? My God!"

"We couldn't find any next of kin info and I knew they worked for you. I'm hoping you have some of that information."

"Wow, this is crazy, Eugene. Give me a second, I'll check their files."

I placed the call on hold and was just numbed by the extremes these invisible players would go to keep the upper hand. They not only have the eyes and ears of the devil, but they have the reach of his hand too. But here's the kicker, each of their personnel files listed the same three next of kin....Raychelle Brown, Reginald Thompson and Sadie Holmes. Each one labeled as cousins. I knew two were related but I didn't know they each lived together in one of those high-rise apartments over on Baker Street. I paid them well but not well enough to live there.

"Eugene, they listed each other as next of kin and lived together at the Heights on Baker Street."

"I'll have to go over to their apartment, maybe something there will help us notify family because otherwise they'll sit at the morgue for a month and then be shipped to the Schuster Parlor for cremation. At any rate, thanks, Ms. Lucy, I'll keep you updated." The call ended.

What will he find at that apartment? Even more so, who were those people? They've worked here all this time and not once has it slipped that they shared an apartment. That was a neither here nor there situation. My focus was now back on the manila envelope. Both ends of it were secured with blue painter's masking tape. The strength of the tape forced me to find a pair of scissors, all of this effort only to find myself the ass of what appeared to be Reggie's final practical joke. He had sealed up a package of Aflac supplemental insurance booklets. The cancer, life, accident, and short-term disability pamphlets were all properly secured. Here I was again with the shame of the prowl thrown back in my face. Frustrated with my catch, I trashed the whole lot of it and started back playing around with the surveillance system. There were several data downloads I needed to gather. In trying to figure out how to get the downloads I started to thumb through the manual and the registration card fell from it. It's amazing how little small things such as that can make the big things click. Something told me to go back to the Aflac booklets, even though I felt weird cyphering back through the trash. Deep down within, I knew I'd overlooked something vital. Reggie's sense of humor was second to none but the boy was lazy with no remorse. There simply was no way in hell he would have taken time to stage those pamphlets in that lockbox just for a down the road laugh.

In dumping the trash on the conference table a contract looking form dropped from the trash that wasn't originally there, and it had Reggie's name on it. At first I didn't get it. It appeared to be just a regular run of the mill adoption form. In reading it two things really stood out. One, this was not just an adoption form, it was a relinquishing of rights signed by both of his parents. Secondly, they relinquished their rights to the old orphanage on Lanberry Drive, "Landing Orphanage". It was closed long before I moved to town but it was housed in an Old South type mansion that the Mayor never outgrew. Reggie was allowed to retain his first name, only he was originally named Reginald Orlando Myles and after it became Reginald Thompson. Attached to the adoption was the missing kid article from the paper and the story ran on the suicide of his father Mr. Myles and then there was one of those damn gold foiled envelopes. The same information was found for Raychelle and Sadie. Only one father went missing and the other two committed suicide. But then there was one attached for Chief Marcelle, he was the only that wasn't adopted by the orphanage but rather he was adopted by Sir Lloyd Wright.

It's crazy that in death I now know more about these folks than I ever knew. The Chief was adopted by a well to do family and into a nice heritage, his father was the glorified Chief Wright. I remember his name from the plaque on the wall in City Hall and a couple other places downtown. I guess he groomed Marcelle for the job and like most children he lived to walk in Daddy's shadow. I'll bet my big toe that he didn't think twice about getting involved in the devilish ways of his father. This was all great news, but even still it didn't explain the need for their deaths.

Marcelle put Eugene on lead in this case no doubt because he knows he won't find anything to make this thing blow up. Somehow we need to play this thing to our advantage, Eugene needs to find this file. I started to call Jayden but stopped when I thought about last night's events, as the phones could be tapped. In glancing at the time and the schedule on the wall it was time to go see Mrs. Pringlaye. I could use one of those tasty sandwich goodies. So far I had kept her out of the loop and I intended to keep it that way. If Raychelle ever did any good it was definitely when she said "we don't know all the players of this game." True facts right there. I slapped the info on the copier and scanned it all to my thumb drive. The old wall safe in the extension building was the first thing to came to mind just in case the place gets ransacked. It's normal for Pringlaye to be nosy but today she gained a double portion of the inquisitive spirit. I started to get a bit frustrated but considering my life was almost destroyed in front of her shop I cooled it.

"Lucy my girl, why didn't you call down here instead of fighting that road?"

"I needed to get out and about, can't let the small stuff hold me down. I've been through worse. Trust me, I have seen worse. How are you doing today, Mrs. Pringlaye?"

"Yeah, I expect such, baby girl. We're sorry and shocked to hear about your workers dying in that accident last night. I always knew that train would claim somebody's life. It's just stupid of these people to see a train coming and try to beat it. What was them children thinking? I know they were probably headed to that damn blasted casino for that crab legs and lobster buffet. Lord, it wasn't worth it and I tell you it's just a shame and a pity."

"Oh, I didn't hear how they died. I just heard it was a car accident and took it like that."

"Yes, child, you must not have watched the news last night, it was nasty. Two cars were hit directly by the train and the others were just from the side effect of speeding I guess."

Exit 39b leads to the casino and it's the front way to the Schuster Hill Estate. At the time of the accident Reggie's car was parked on the side of the road. Then it hit me that I didn't see that pretty black Jeep Cherokee of his parked across the street anymore. I'm sure it was there last night but now it's gone.

"I imagine the bodies were mangled apart. I remember when I was a child a train hit a family in a station wagon and it just tore their bodies apart. They had a closed casket with the body parts placed in body bags. The folks didn't know what parts belonged to who. My God this just too sad. You know them children grew up in that old orphanage and were never adopted. They were just like brothers and sisters."

"No, ma'am, I didn't know that. This really is sad. It sounds like they had a tough life."

"Yeah, times were so bad back then that folks were coming from the east to the west turning their kids over to the orphanage. Their main goal was to secure meals for the little ones. Of course they could never see the children anymore. Some folks committed suicide, worried by the grief I suspect. The Mayor's family did a great thing for this community by starting such a place. I hear just about all of those children went on to be successful, can't say I knew any of them except those three that worked for you. But they did good for you, right?"

"Yes, ma'am, I'm certainly going to miss them. I wonder if there will be a funeral ceremony or anything?"

In sitting there listening to her talk my mind churned a million times over. She answered some of the whys but still left me in the dark.

"Well, I'm going step over and check in with Jayden, Mrs. Pringlaye, and if I hear any updates I'll be sure to let you know. Have a good day and I'll send one of the volunteers over to pick up the plates around 3:30, is that fine?"

"Okay, child, you have a good day as well and yes 3:30 will be fine. Tell Jayden I said hello, he didn't come over for breakfast this morning, you two must have had a long night."

I smiled nervously and said "bye" while exiting the door. I vaguely remembered seeing her among the crowd of frantic people that surrounded the car last night. The old lady probably thought he and I had played hide the hatchet all evening. I only wish that was all our evening entailed instead of dark spots, gunshots, dead bodies and more secrets. Oh, how the precious secrets unfold.

"Ms. Lucy!" rang all around the shop upon my first step in the door. These guys always know how to make my ego stand as tall as Goliath. As usual it was all eyes on me. I smiled in the direction of the fellas and continued walking to Jayden's office. It was closed. I knew I should have knocked before entering but a girlfriend gets the privilege to be a little abrasive sometimes. I opened that door and saw the true face of death as he lived and breathed. The Richter scale on my life had been shocked.

"Heyyyy, Jayden," I called as my eyes quickly scanned the room like a robot, only to find Jayden not present.

"Please forgive me for being so rude."

He caught me totally off guard but I needed to make sure it didn't show. Truth is the man gives me heart quakes every time I'm in his presence. Chief Marcelle sat there looking even more vindictive and evil than usual. My heart was pounding -- for real this is the boogeyman.

"Good morning, Ms. Lucy. My condolences for the loss of your employees. They were some pretty fine folks. My son spoke highly of them."

"Oh yes. This is quite the shocker. It's equally sad to know they are no longer amongst our presence. I pray their deaths were quick and that they didn't have to lay in the dark begging God for His sweet mercy to prevail."

"They didn't see it coming until it hit them I'm sure, and by that time they were likely dead upon impact. Trains almost never miss their target."

"Target you say?"

"If you're caught on the track when he arrives, you're that target. It's almost an automatic bullseye."

94

All before now he'd sat there appearing proud and mighty relaxed in his seat. It was at this moment that I shook him a bit. I saw him when he took in a big swallow and recourse for words. Our eyes sat toe to toe when we spoke. Each eye revealed the truth and told the other what the tongues refused to say.

Like the strike of lightning Jayden appeared at the door. He had a look of frustration on his face upon glaring my direction.

"Sorry about the wait, Chief. Umm, wow. Lucy, how long have you been here?"

"Hey. I've been here for about five minutes discussing the train accident with the Chief. I didn't want anything, I was just checking in. I'll let you two get back to your business. Have a good day."

"No need to rush off, Ms. Lucy, I was just getting Mr. Jayden's statement of your own accident last night. I was going to stop by the foundation to speak with you. Since you're here already I may as well shoot two birds with one stone. That's if you are not in a terrible hurry."

My mind immediately went back to Reggie's car being parked across the street. I wondered if Jayden's cameras caught who drove it away that night.

"Well, it's not much of a statement, all I did was park my car and opened the door and watched it get torn from my car and thrown down the road. The black Suburban or Escalade continued on down the road with its music blaring with no damns given. The windows were limo tinted black and I didn't catch the license plate. Just about everyone downtown surrounded my car after it happened. Hopefully someone's phone snapped a picture."

"Yeah, hopefully so. Well you two have a good day. I'll let you know when I know more. Be careful, there are some ruthless people that travel these streets."

As he exited the door, he glanced back in our direction then slithered away like a garter snake. Jayden followed behind him while signaling my way to keep quiet. He stood there at the door until the Chief was out of sight. Then proceeded to lock the door and pull out some sort of metal detector thingy and went around the office like a crazed man waiting for it to beep. Thankfully there was nothing to be found.

"You can't trust that joker."

"Did you really think he would bug your office?"

"Yes, we can't be careful enough. Let your guard down, Lucy, and you end up kissing a train."

"You heard already, huh?"

"Yeah, Eugene stopped by this morning after he had breakfast and told me everything. So what you doing down this way?"

Briefly I had forgotten what I stopped by to tell him. Then it began to click again.

"Where's your laptop?" I asked.

"Upstairs. Why?"

"Come on, let's get to it. I got something to show you. After having him here, this office is giving me the heebie-jeebies. You might need to do a sage cleanse."

"Girl, you're crazy to come on. My mom is here so you'll get a chance to finally meet her."

We went out the back door of the office and up the stairs to the apartment. He called out for his mom, but she didn't answer. After going from room to room he concluded she must be visiting with Pringlaye. We set up on the sofa and I plugged my flash drive into the computer and showed him the files. He sat there reading. Likely about as shocked as I was when I first saw it.

"Where'd you get this?"

"Reggie gave it to me. I found it in his desk bundled in some pamphlets in an old lockbox. It's like this was an insurance plan for him only he didn't get a chance to cash in."

"What do you plan to do with it?"

"Eugene said that he would have to do a search of their apartment to try and find a next of kin relative to inform of their deaths. I think that Marcelle has already swept the place clean of anything that will do any good. I need to get a copy of this placed in that apartment. Then we need to do a search for the parents and maybe get it anonymously submitted to the FBI."

"Lucy, calm down. Have you thought this out clearly? You're almost at the point of no return. If you do this the wheels will really start to roll. Are you ready for the thunder of this storm? I got to tell you, I'm not so sure if it's worth the constant shoulder watching that will come."

"Jayden, this has to stop somewhere. I'm willing if you're willing. Think about it and we'll talk later. I put a copy of the file on your computer just in case you need a second read. Like I said, we'll talk later about this."

I left for the old city library in search of the answers no one else could provide me. Growing up I read a lot of murder mysteries and often the best criminals left behind plain sight clues. I came looking for just that. Once I arrived in the library, I walked around the three-story building reading over titles as if I knew the object of my search. After a while it became increasingly apparent that I needed to seek assistance. I had passed a nice young man several times restocking the shelves, and by the fifth awkward smile I raised my hand.

"Excuse me, but good morning, I'm looking for any books and articles on the history of Schuster's Hill and Landing, can you direct me to that area? Also, what do you know about the history of the Mayor's Old Orphanage Estate? That place looks to have such a great history and character and I'd love to just know more."

"I can help you with that, my name is Samuel, I'm actually a historian intern from the University. Schuster's Landing and Schuster's Hill actually share the same history except for one fine detail. But follow me, all the good information we have is in the basement."

"Lead the way, Captain."

He smiled in my direction.

"So what's that fine detail?" I asked.

He entered the elevator and held the door for me. "DNA."

The elevator slammed shut and shook quickly downward in a way that seemed dangerous then it leveled out. I quickly grabbed for the wall railing while wondering immediately if Jayden might be right in wondering if this is really worth it. I'm running around here in old ass elevators risking my life for what? It'd be a shame for me to die now from a 50-year-old elevator given the events of my last 24 to 48 hours.

"Sorry, I forgot to tell you to hold to the rail for a second, these old elevators act like death traps."

"No problem. So DNA is the fine detail? I don't get it. Does that stand for something other than what I think?"

"Nothing really interesting other than Mayor Ralph Schuster and Big Slim "Big Slim" Schuster who owns the Schuster Hill Parlor are close cousins. Apples from the same tree if you will. Big Slim is the great great granddaughter of the town's founding father Mayor Emery Lowell Schuster by a Creole slave woman named Ms. Jenny Woods. He had such a great love for Jenny that he set her and her family free to live and own Schuster Hill for all generations. The white community didn't approve but who would stand up against the richest man of the South?"

From the outside you couldn't tell the building had such an extensive basement and though neat and tidy you could tell it lacked frequent visitors. We walked a country mile until we finally made it to a small area in the back of the building to a black brownish old trunk.

"That Hill land turned out to be a better portion of property than he left behind for his home heirs. That's pretty much the history of the two towns, well the Cliff Note version. But I didn't bring you down here for that. You asked about the old orphanage and I just so happened to have found some old pictures and a journal of an orphan that lived there in the early years. I haven't had a chance to document it to the library but you're free to look over it. It's probably worth your read."

"Thanks so much, Samuel."

I sat there on the floor with my back to the wall glancing through the pictures. Nothing significant had been captured. It's funny that the pictures at the orphanage only documented what appeared to be the lives of three children growing up with their parents. There was no abundance of other children even in the background. My attention was again placed on the reddish leather-bound journal from Ernesto Beauteet. He was 12 years old when he arrived at the orphanage - scared and confused.

"Momma said I'm sorry my son, but this is best I can see to do. I pray God will help you forgive me someday. Every day for almost two years I've thought I had a bad dream only but I soon realize I'm in hell."

This journal entry told me this wasn't supposed to ever be found and it wouldn't make it any further than a fire if I left it here. There I sat stuck in the dilemma of knowing what to do but still wanting to do the right thing. This kid was so detailed and crafted with intrigue that he'd no doubt come looking for this relic. I didn't really give him my name but it's not like he couldn't pick my face from a lineup. I scanned the room for cameras, packed the book and one of the pictures in my purse and made like a ghost in the wind. While I waited for the elevator, to my left I noticed the exit only sign. The entrance brought me to the back of the library and right in sight of the orphanage front door. The thought did come to mind to strike out running but my better senses thought of the attention that would bring. What's taboo about me taking a nice stroll along the sidewalk? By the time I got to my car my heart had anticipated Marcelle to appear out of nowhere with cuffs in hand. I know the level of wrongness to my plight, but I just could not leave this behind. It had to be some sort of puzzle piece to make all this appear sensible.

After sitting there for a while and no cops showed I decided to go back to the center. The thought of what I would read was driving me almost insane. If you saw how erratic I was driving, you'd agree. Praise God I caused no accidents and didn't have the cops trailing behind me. Once I was at the center I didn't try to get in the building . I just started reading, there simply was no time to waste.

"Same thing every night, three knocks at the door then in comes a light in the darkness pulling my nightshirt up and fingering at my body. The smell of bacon grease infuses the room. I know to roll over to my stomach and to keep quiet or be choked to an inch of life's drawstring and even still he forces himself into my body. Some nights I lie there in the darkness looking at the world I imagine is waiting on me to run away towards. My thoughts help me to feel past the pain being forced on me. I wish some god or spirit would come to save me from this trauma I'm knowing at the hands of these people. At the end of it all he forever whispers in my ear, "He's been here." After he's been long gone the Misses appears like clockwork every morning at 5 a.m. with her whip in hand. Why don't they just fucking kill me and be done."

I got insanely pissed off reading this journal, the rage made me cry to myself. My heart just couldn't understand how these people would find it in their hearts to be so wicked to a child. My own son came to mind, Uncle Buck and Aunt Shelia will be here in a few weekends with the return of my little Remi. With all the trouble shifting around this place my son had sadly faded from my mind's view. I hadn't forgotten him but I really had gotten used to not having my baby in the mix of this mess.

I stuffed the journal back into my purse and pulled myself back together to face this day. After all, I need all my strength to step in the shoes of the three. I don't know how or why but I keep getting the strength to restart this journey daily. I'm so used to giving up and running away from my troubles but that hasn't been true since my arrival here in Schuster. It's like all my life I never really belonged but here even in the midst of death, corruption, and the grave I know I belong. As scared and challenged that I am of what tomorrow may or may not hold, I rise to the call.

Standing there at the head of the conference table glancing at what remained of my staff I whispered a prayer to God within. Not asking for the battle to be over but for the strength to endure even these troubled times.

"Good morning everyone. I don't know if everyone has heard, but last night we lost Raychelle, Sadie, and Reggie to a train accident. Out near the casino."

Everyone sat with a look of serene understanding on their face, the three AmeriCorps Volunteers shed a few tears, but Mr. Riley and Mr. Theodore sat there with neutral faces that puzzled my spirit. Could they be in on this mess too?

"I know the task at hand is going to be tough but if we're all in this thing together it will be a success. As you all know I'm here if at any time things feel exasperating. At any rate, here's what we got. I'm going to fill in with the classes, I'll need someone to work the front office basically just answering the phones and performing housekeeping duties. Just until I can hire someone permanently for the position."

"I'll work in the front office, Ms. Lucy"

"Perfect! Thanks, Raymond. Okay, Becky and Lauren, you guys will continue to work the conjoined classroom, I'll just be the facilitator but actually the baton is in your hands. This will actually be a great time to really put your educations and experience to work. Hone in on your strengths and expel your weaknesses. Everything will be alright. Are you guys up to it?"

The two agreed with looks of delight. This might have been their first time to really feel included within the foundation with any true degree of freedom. Truth be told, Raychelle wasn't too keen on the volunteers, her insecurities prevented them from gaining the true experience that should have been granted previously and her insecurities always overflowed to Sadie. But then again when you're doing wrong you can't afford to chance the revealing of the face behind the mask.

"Well it sounds like we're all set. If there are aren't any questions let's get out there and make it happen. Raymond, you go ahead and go get yourself acclimated with Reggie's office and I'll check in with you here shortly."

I don't know about tomorrow but if it's anything like what I just experience today all will be well. Everyone exited the room with their high spirits shining through brightly. This group right here are the real dream champions. During mealtime we took a moment for prayer as usual. Pringlaye's sandwiches are always a treat from heaven but little Samuel Ellis shocked everyone when he walked up to the podium and took Mr. Riley's hand. He beckoned him down to his 9-year-old height. We sat there wondering what was to come, I thought maybe he needed to be excused to the restroom. What happened next astonished not only his peers but even we adults stood in awe. Mr. Riley handed the child the microphone and he began to recite the 23rd Psalm and he ended the prayer with, "Father, bless their souls even as they abide in your bosom." You'd expect something like that from a preacher's kid but he's no P.K. Lord, if my chest didn't press out tall yesterday didn't exist. The child said 'abide in your bosom,' I tell your children will shock you every time. He took his seat with all eyes on him…he had a mic drop moment. The rest of the evening went smoother than fresh butter. The child anointed our hearts and blessed the devil out.

The drive home that evening was peaceful. My Remi called me speaking in Spanish. All thanks to his Uncle Buck. It seemed like I hadn't spoken to my champ in years despite talking every Saturday for almost a month. Before the little sport left, he told me, "I'm a big boy and big boys don't call their mommy every night. I'll call you every Saturday. Is that okay with you, Mommy?"

I smiled and promised to hold him to his word fully expecting him to drop his end of the bargain, but sure enough my little man has done just that. With all the drama I have found myself in at the center this plan has worked out wonderfully. Fortunately for me Jayden had left me a healthy helping of his famous shrimp and grits. I pigged out and sat there in the living room reading more of the journal. I wondered whatever became of this young man. Did he run away like he planned, or did they ultimately kill him? His spirit appeared strong despite being treated so gruesomely. I must have nodded off a bit because I jolted out of my sleep at the sound of my phone vibrating roughly on the coffee table. It sounded like a mini grinder. I didn't look to see who was calling, the noise just needed to stop.

"Lucy, girl, I need you to check something out for me. I got a call from Randy at the coroner's office. His office will be bringing the bodies of the three to us to be cremated and disposed at the expense of the railroad."

"The railroad?"

"Yeah yeah, whenever there's an accident involving the train the railroad steps in and takes care of things despite who's at fault…but that's not important. When Deputy Coroner Cecil called me he never mentioned any bullet holes in the people. Only how he had to work hard to match the arms and heads with the correct bodies of the two girls. So you know what that means?"

"They're probably still in the mines, huh?"

"Nawl, not likely, well not above the ground. Marcelle and whoever he's working with aren't stupid. But we've said enough on these here phones. I'll have Ellis to email you pictures of the remains when they get here."

"Okay, I'll keep an eye out for that email."

"Oh okay. one more thing. Lucy-Chile. I had a dream about those two men working for you. I can't quite call it all just yet but you can trust them. They not regular men."

"You talking about Riley and Theodore? Not regular men, are you telling me we have angels posing as men here in Schuster as well?"

"Chile, you funny but if you want to call it that way, them men gonna be your angels, just watch it out. And you'd be amazed at what's lurking and creeping amongst us here in Schuster. I come from the line of a Creole Voodoo Priestess and a semi ruthless rich white man. Possibilities are limitless, child. I saw you coming to this town long before you ever knew it existed and I'll tell you one other thing, Lucy, you gonna make a damn good leader and that condition you claiming ain't never been yours to hold. Ever wonder why you don't need more and more pills? Come see me tomorrow, I have much to tell you. You mustn't forget to remember tomorrow's hope can fade yesterday's heartache. Sleep well, chile."

The call ended with me being confused about what she was talking about. Sometimes Big Slim's word is a bit too riddled. I'm anxious to get back with her tomorrow. The last thing she said was straight from my mother's book but I don't remember telling her so.

I looked over at the time, it was 11:30. I had been trying to read through the journal and gain some more insight into the life of this young man but from what I could see it was only a record of forced sex with either the orphanage owner or his son and the wife's revenge. I was expecting more. I needed more but unfortunately it didn't have that to offer me.

The recourse of today had me exhausted surprisingly in a great way. You couldn't have asked for a better day, things never missed a hitch. It was like the three never existed, everyone just fell in place and made it a success. However, now that she mentioned the fellas they were extra cool with the deaths of the three despite working so closely with them over the years. They showed no emotion at all. I rolled around under the covers, whispered a prayer to God and went out like a light.

I awakened out of my sleep by this light but loud thud from downstairs. Living alone has heightened my senses when it comes to noise. Even the smallest noise can waken me. My first attention was my barricaded door. I needed to make sure all was in place. I reached under the pillow for my big sister and then for my phone for the camera app turning on the lights and scanning all the cameras for the intruder. But I saw no one in the cameras and there was nothing out of place in either of the yards. Seeing no one did nothing for my anxiety. I lay there in bed for an hour awaiting some Grimm spirit to appear and snatch my soul but finally I drifted back to sleep.

That night I dreamed the FBI stormed the foundation with both Riley and Theodore as the agents in charge. They arrested me for the murders of the three and of Chief Marcelle. Everything seemed so real, I remembered I kept pinching myself trying to wake up only to find I was stuck pleading my innocence only to be thrown in a dark pit similar to the mines where I kept hearing Reggie pleading for mercy. Things were just about to get worse when my alarm started to blare. Praise God for the alarms. I woke up drenched in enough sweat to think someone had tried drowning me in my sleep. After laying there for five minutes or so trying to make sense of it all I walked over to stop the alarm. With all that had happened around me, I would be lying if I said this dream didn't create a new pause in my spirit.

I finally got Big Slim's email and was not one bit shocked to see that the faces in the pictures were not the people I worked with for almost three years. Instead what laid there were likely three innocent people who got caught in the triangle. The remains were turned over to Big Slim, and due to the conditions of the remains the claiming period was reduced to three days. The cremation period will have to be expedited as well; the normal processing period was suspended. This situation always appears grim, but it always has a way of working out. We have to just take this pizza one slice at a time. Nonetheless, seeing those pictures did nothing but confirmed the reach of this influence. Remaining humble and operating in the dark and keeping quiet is our only real advantage to stringing this crime scene together. So as I sat at the table eating my cereal I weighed my options. Then it became clear I hadn't a real one. These folks were like that of the mob or some meticulous invisible group of serial killers. A day is coming where I'll have to choose to stand on the battleground for what I believe. I'll be ready.

A knock at the back door snapped me out of my thoughts. I sat there smiling within knowing who was knocking and unlocking the door. There was no need to look over my shoulder for confirmation. After all, what stranger has a key to unlock my door.

"Jayden, to what do I owe this early morning pleasure? And that key is supposed to be for emergencies only, sir."

"Oh, but emergency it is, Miss Lucy." That dark sultry voice didn't match at all to Jayden. Still I sat there continuing to eat my breakfast while the voice stood calmly not more than eight feet from me. My mind didn't race and my heart didn't lose control.

"Why are you here in my house? Did you come to kill me and lay my body on a train track? Or even better leave me begging for my life in an old mineshaft? Or will I slip and fall to my death down some whimsical stairwell?" All the while continuing to eat my cereal.

"No, none of that. I come to make you a life offer."

"Life offer, what, join you or die?"

"Ms. Lucy, there's worse things in life than dying. In fact, dying is the easy way. Nonetheless, dying is the fool's way out. I expect a yes or you'll sit on this hill and watch it all crumble. Building by building, life by life until you beg me to be the reaper." The man gave me a great deal of fear to consider, a mighty ultimatum but yet the spirit of calm kept my soul still.

"A man with a master plan standing behind me makes me itch just a wee bit. Come have a seat. look me in the eyes. Don't you police get off on reading eye messages?"

"Fair enough, I can sit with you. But I don't need to read your eyes, Miss Lucy. I know you try to be a puzzling woman, but yet you ain't no puzzle."

He sat directly across from me at the table gazing into my eyes as if he were mesmerized to their delight. I looked upon him calmly. Something deep within me wanted to be freaked out but the greater portion of self knew that all would be well. I sat there with my Three Sisters strapped to my inner thigh just waiting on the top of this can to pop off.

"Marcelle, make this interesting. I understand your guarantees, but you shouldn't expect me not to make a warranty claim. What are you seeking from me? And before you start, put my damn key on the table and Jayden better be okay. Believe me or no, I can put an end this to this charade."

He did as I demanded and chuckled lightly.

"Lucy, you are a funny lady. Sitting here acting like this deck is stacked in your favor. This isn't that foundation of kids you run. The keys of demand are not in your hands. But yet you pretend like you're in control. I like that in a woman. Look at you all pumped up with circumstance I bet you'd tremble under a good stroke."

"Come on with the lowdown, Marcelle." My impatience started to rear its head.

"Okay. We want you to pick up where they had to drop off. That financial boot camp class of yours will continue. No hiccups will be accepted. That's the lowdown. I expect you to make the right decision really soon."

With no further words he got up and walked back to the door.

"Use the front door. Most of my trash goes out that way. Back doors are reserved for people I can trust."

"Trust and life have nothing to do with the other. I'll be expecting your call. For your sake I hope it's the right answer. Oh yeah one more thing, tell your little boy toy to do a better job of keeping up with his keys. There are a lot of maniacs walking around us in this small place."

"I guess you're the leader. Exit my home."

"Remember your options, Ms. Lucy, wouldn't want your little Remy to know a life without you."

Sitting there calmer than calm in the face of this adversity took balls I didn't know I had grown. This single moment told me what to do. There was no further need for a mental discussion. This man threatened my whole life, not some but the whole damn story. I don't know how or when, but he will feed the boneyard. The straws had been drawn and it's time to make the mountain shake. Since the very beginning I knew who I needed to call. Some ten years ago I vowed to never deal in black blood again. But here I am wanting to do just what he prophesied I would do all those years ago. I can hear him now. "One day, daughter, you'll call and I'll have no problem answering." Soon he just might be known as a true prophet. Not before I go have a word with Big Slim. I'm surprised she hasn't called me back to see when I'd be on my way there. I'm still a bit taken back by those pictures. Today's journey is still a bit sketchy to me. Marcelle has entered my home without permission and with a key. Only this key isn't Jayden's, it's from under the plant out back. That bastard just knew I'd get flustered at the mention of Jayden's name but not today, devil. Even still, something just doesn't sit right with my soul. I can't touch it but something in the atmosphere just ain't right.

As I drove and fought with old county 8 this thought crossed my mind. True, he had been in Jayden's office, but he didn't get what he wanted from Jayden and he didn't get it from me either. Now he's trying to recruit me for the grand old position, or I am to start watching my allies die. There's pressure being applied but where's the diamond?

"Hey, Darryl, it's Lucy. I need the doors at the house rekeyed. I texted pictures of the locks. If you can I need one key to work on all the locks. Just give me a call when you get this message. Thanks."

Darryl didn't answer the phone but that's not too uncommon, people do get busy or sleep, I thought to myself. The further I got down the road the stranger the drive got. Something is really up, I just can't seem to place my finger on it. I started seeing the flashing of red and blue ambulance lights in the far distance in the direction of the parlor. Still I thought nothing of the sighting. It could be for a funeral attendant, people do pass out at the funerals quite often. Only as I got closer to the estate and at the foot of the driveway, I could see that it was at the grand old house. Didn't nobody have to say nothing -- the cold chill that coursed down my spine said it all. My thoughts immediately turned to her. Things got cloudy, then in my mind I saw the worry in Ellis' face that night in the living room. Those two knew something the rest of us brushed off as just worry. While sitting there watching the ambulance lights twirl my 17th birthday fell fresh in my view. Here I am sitting in the car paralyzed not knowing what to do or think just like back then. Sure, things could have been simple and not as grim as I was imagining but my heart told me death had been here. I sat there with my foot on the brake channeling in between the past and the right now. I kept seeing my childhood home and all the police surrounding it like little ants and the flashing red ambulance lights. As I can remember it, one of the neighbors pointed at my car then an officer came running in my direction.

"Ma'am, are you Marie Antoinette Martinez?"

"Yes, sir, I am". I remember my voice cracked automatically. I didn't know what, but I knew it wasn't good.

"And do you live here with your parents?"

"Yes, sir."

"Ma'am, I'm sorry to tell you but your home was burglarized, and your parents were murdered."

"My mom and dad are dead?"

That's all I can remember from that moment in time. To tell the truth I have tried for years to forget that time and until today it had been filed away in the back of my head. I needed to get inside and see what's going on but my legs refused to cooperate. Pulling myself to face reality seemed impossible. Marcelle and his words flashed across my mind. One by one he said. I started to put the car in reverse and leave but in my rearview I saw Jayden tracing up the driveway. He streaked past the car and up the steps into the house. When the door opened the agony escaped to the outside world. What a sound, Ellis wailed like any child would at the face of her mother's transition. Still I sat there on the brakes paralyzed. That was enough to break my mind a true lesson for the heart but I heard her voice just as clear as if she sat in the car with me.

"Chile, death ain't got no sting for the righteous. Him only doing what he was designed to do. Death is just the door to your next life. Now go help my people, be strong for me."

You would have thought I would have started running but I got off the brakes, put the car in park and watched as they loaded her into the coroner's van. Neither Ellis nor Jayden came to the door to see her leave. Mr. Lyles stood in the doorway, he actually assisted the guys in loading her into the vehicle. He shook their hands and smiled in my direction. His smile of fire golden teeth brought me hints of comfort. This day he was no longer weird. Now, I just didn't want to accept her transition. I found myself starting to collapse and sob on the steering wheel. I couldn't tell you the last time I actually cried. Tears in my family were a sign of weakness. He opened the passenger door, sat down and grabbed hold of my shoulder.

"Lucy, have you ever known an apple tree to bear apples in the winter season?"

"No, sir, I can't say I do."

"Me neither, baby girl. I was about your age when I came to know Big Slim and then little Ellis who was about five years old. Even then she was a mighty fortress. I lived on my pappy's plantation down in the landing. Until the day an old tall pelican told me he couldn't stomach a nigger like me."

"Like you? Your dad said that? What did you do?"

"No, I had a white daddy, my uncle Mr. Rodger Schuster was the pelican. I could pass. Hell, I was passing for white until Mister Dean died. Up until his death he never outrightly acknowledged me as his son but he made sure I had the best on the farm and nobody ever messed me around. The people hated my existence blacks and whites alike. At that time I didn't know about Big Slim until his death. I was present at his will reading when Oldman George Hopkins read out aloud to my son Lyles Dean Williams. I leave you the plantation house on the Northside of the Schuster Landing Farm. It was his home and the only place I knew as home. I lived in a room on the first floor. Not too many knew much about my true heritage but a few of the sharecroppers but they wouldn't dare breathe a word out loud. The rest of his message was in the form of a long letter that I still keep close to my heart. My daddy loved me even though he had to keep me a secret. My dear mother died birthing me, he couldn't forget me so he raised me. That same day my world went up in flames. You talk about a fire… that old place burned like old paper. Hate is a fierce contender, Ms. Lucy. I was kicked off the plantation estate I had grown to know as home and dropped off on old county 8. I didn't have to walk too long before drove up Big Slim in her Bessie. She whipped around in the road and hit that ole beat-up green hearse in the ass and I been here ever since. She's been there for me till today."

"Lyles, I just didn't have enough time with her. What happened? I spoke with her last night around close to midnight I believe? She sounded fine."

"No time to us is ever enough. Not even a lifetime. However, she insisted that we go back down to the old mine last night to search around for those bodies. After news got around of those three dying where we knew they didn't die, she got curious. We would have included y'all last night, but she wanted you and Jayden to rest. We got down to the area where we stood that night and didn't find a hint of nothing. No blood stains or anything. All of a sudden there was an explosion, everything got dark and dusty and the way we came was blocked. I started to panic but Big Slim locked into my arm and we found another way. All thanks goes to her childhood knowledge of the place and those night vision

113

goggles. Somehow we wound around to the front entrance of the mine and almost walked right up on the Chief and the Mayor, we must have arrived at the last minute because they got in their cars and drove off and never once noticed our presence. Thankfully they were in their cars otherwise they'd have heard us hacking the dust clean from our lungs. The walk was long we didn't make it back to the grand house until around 3 a.m. this morning. Last I spoke with her she was headed for a shower and then to bed. This morning one of the Lil grands went to bring her breakfast in bed and she never woke up."

"Wow, who would have known our last talk would be our last talk?"

"She did. She and Ellis have been speaking in riddles for weeks now. I walked in on a couple of their conversations with her telling Ellis, 'baby, it's getting late in the evening and I don't have a choice.' I never thought much into it. She had even been preparing me as well. Usually she and I worked alongside each other but since the summer she's been getting Ellis to take her place on most of the preps."

"Lyles, we have got to be strong for her and the family."

"True we do. Be strong for her? Those are her words."

"I know, she spoke them not too long ago. Come, let us go in the house and do just that. "

"You ain't telling me nothing, Big Slim gonna have her say even in death."

We smiled and entered the house, it felt strange already. The family was all situated in the foyer -around the organ. Ellis was playing an uplifting contemporary hymn. The little ones were on the floor gazing upon their mother and Jayden. The song said, "I just want to Praise You Forever and ever." Simple but heartfelt words touched the spirit. My God, I had never heard Ellis play the organ nor Jayden sing, but this song was befitting to our moment. Weeping and sorrow endure only for a moment but Joy comes in the morning light. Despite all the confusion and frustration our souls got even more acquainted with peace. I felt like we gave her soul a proper send-off, doing what she loved the best, Praising the Lord.

When the music stopped the children went charging up to hug Jayden and kissed their mother on the cheek then quickly disappeared upstairs. They'd been trained to leave the adults to their business without a word of direction from their mother. We stood there awaiting a word from Ellis.

"My mom loved everyone in this house, some of you are bound by blood but she believed and taught me neither blood nor water really mattered. Love is the binder. Lucy, you are forever a part of this family." My eyes watered. "Now I didn't want her getting involved with the matters of townsfolk. We know the consequences of such actions. I have three children up there to raise up to be strong men and I don't want no point of their existence blemished by those townsfolks trying to play God. What we are going to do is band together and figure this thing out. In the meantime, it has to run its course. Now, Lucy, you call him up and give him your answer." Jayden and Lyles looked in my direction confused. I looked bewildered as to how she knew just what to say.

"Who do you need to call, Lucy? What's going on?"

"Marcelle came in my home this morning with a key to the backdoor and tried to lead me to believe it was your key and that you were in danger. I thought he was you so I never even looked back in his direction. He didn't try to hurt me or anything. Basically, he gave me one option, join his team or watch all around me crumble. I'm not about to join him. I realize now more than ever before that either I got to shit or get off the pot. I didn't come all this way to give up and bow down to the unknown forces. He warned me that everything I loved would die all around me and I would be begging him to be the reaper. Guys, I sat there in the midst of all his guarantees of harm and evil intentions but there was no fear in my heart. I know this trouble can't last forever and, Ellis, I'm with you one hundred percent. Ladies and gentlemen, we are at war and we will fight and we will conquer."

We might have sat there for another hour or so talking things through. Jayden looked upon me with admiration in his eyes. He didn't say much but I felt the love of his fear even when we joined hands and Ellis led us in prayer. When he and I prepared to leave, the strange factor reappeared. I kept expecting Big Slim to follow behind us to the front door and to stand on the porch smiling and waving us away until our next visit. We stood beside my car with Jayden talking and me still looking back every so often towards the porch for her presence. We hugged and did our "until later" greeting and got in our separate cars. I sat there behind the wheel smiling even in the midst of this valley of the shadow of death. Then ironically death texted me. The phone flashed with a message from Marcelle: "have you made the right decision?" I texted back "yes and my answer is no. Me and mine will follow the righteous path." He didn't reply but I fully understand that a silenced gun though quiet still discharges lethal hot lead. If I'm to walk this righteous way I must walk it fearfully strong.

Despite being on constant edge the next few days went fairly well. Ellis decided to have a small quiet ceremony for Big Slim that included the gang of us and a few select townsfolk. Good thing the ceremony was hosted in the De'Aria Room. Word got around and I know some three or four hundred people filled the capacity. Among those who appeared in came Mayor Ralph Schuster. I didn't imagine he'd rear his face. One simply never can tell how others are truly feeling just by looking at them. However, that fact didn't stop me from trying to glimmer Mayor Ralph's true feelings from gazing into his blue graying eyes. Ellis asked me to sing one of her mother's favorite songs, Precious Lord. My my my, talk about accompany, she did it. Ellis played that organ like it was her first language. The devilish side of me said the Mayor only came to make sure she was really dead. But the man teared up a little bit. A many crocodile tear has the devil shed but even his once angelic presence still knows not repentance.

It was a nice service, quite a few state officials came out to pay their respects, everyone regarded her and the family highly. This woman took the cards she was dealt and lived a grand life that touched hearts both far and near. Her grandsons did a wonderful job of ushering no doubt as their granny had taught them. I had really forgotten about the older son Jon, he was away in college. I guess music must have run in the Schuster genes because Lyles was on the piano doing a grand job and from what I have heard about the white Schuster's they are nothing short of maestros. A few of their children are acclaimed pianists. I've witnessed little Julian playing around with organ in the house. At the close of the service Ellis spoke a few words over her mother but what stuck with me was Big Slim's own words, "Life is long, Life is short, Life is Hell, Life is Heavenly, this Life can be whatever you will it to be so long as you're willing to the Good Lord." I had heard this many times before now but today I guess it really started to make sense. Seeing this view of my loved one laid out resting in the presence of her Maker only gave me yet another source of strength on which to stand firmly. There were no cries of regret ringing around the place, only the gathering of love for Big Slim "Big Slim" Schuster. It was indeed a service befitting this fine queen.

Towards the conclusion Lyles replaced Ellis on the organ while she, the boys, Jayden and I lined up at the exit. I've never been hugged so much in my life. But for the memory of Big Slim I'd stand there a thousand times over. In between hugs Jayden got a chance to whisper in my ear.

"I mailed a copy of that file to Eugene from a Jane Doe address. He should be getting it either today or tomorrow. I even mailed a copy to the paper and the train company. We should be getting some action in town soon."

I nodded in agreement. But thought to myself this probably won't go anywhere. These guys have a reach that seems to extend just as close if not further than God Himself. In that instant my cell started to vibrate. It was a call from Shelia. The crowd was thinning fast so I just ignored the call with full intentions to just call back from the car. Next the phone was vibrating again, she went against the grain and left a voicemail. Immediately I knew something was up. With no further delay I stepped out the line and took a seat on the pew to listen to the message.

"Lucy, call me when you get this message. Buck has had a massive stroke and has a hemorrhage on the brain. He's in a coma, it doesn't look good. Please get here. God, I'd feel so much better with you here. I know he'll listen to you."

I know this has nothing to do with Marcelle and his goons but damn if my life isn't getting turned upside down right now. I tried returning her call but it went straight to her unestablished mailbox. It was time to get to her. By that time

119

Jayden recognized the concern on my face and joined me on the pew. I told him the bad news and started to exit the building.

"Lucy, go home, get your bags packed and I'll pick you up and drop you at the airport. Do you want me to fly out there with you?"

"You're a true godsend but I'll be fine. Just put a prayer up for Uncle Buck. I'll see you in a bit, I should be ready in about 25 to 30 minutes."

We embraced in the hallway of the parlor like a couple for the first time ever. I could feel his calm exuding from his muscles to my alarmed spirit. It felt good to exhale in his arms. I have no words to explain it but it's like my strength had just been kickstarted. Maybe this is what true love feels like. He kissed my neck and turned to get back with the family.

"Be safe on the road and I'll see you in 20 minutes."

"Okay, thanks again."

"Lucy, what are you thanking me for?"

"I just thank you for being you."

He smiled and went back inside the parlor to rejoin the family. He calmed my butterfly. But that moment was short-lived. The first thing I spotted out the door was Chief Marcelle's black Tahoe. It was like the monster knew I'd be in this spot at this very time. The black-tinted driver's side window rolled down as I got closer to my car which he conveniently parked next to. He pretended to extend his sympathies but the words taunted me.

"Funny thing about humans. No matter who we are or what we claim to be. We expire. Ashes to ashes but dust to the dust we are sure to return. It'll do you good to remember that, Ms. Lucy. I'm going to miss that old relic just a wee bit."

A response to his disgust was necessary but I caught my tracks and did the next best thing. I smiled at the maggot and walked on my way. The window rolled back up and he left a bit of rubber on the parking lot. Someday I hope to mow this man down like a simple blade of grass.

A metallic blue Mini Cooper sat to the right side of my driveway. It didn't place a hold on any particular person in my head when I turned onto the drive but the minute, I parked the car two familiar slender built souls stepped out. So caught up in my own thoughts that once I recognized them, I immediately thought of the foundation. How can I be leaving town and not have someone in charge during my absence? There wasn't much time to waste but for these two a minute or so was definitely available. While taking a seat on the front porch I beckoned for their approach. I didn't know why they were paying me a visit but from their movements and exuding vibes my nerves seemed to be in comfort.

"Hello, fellas, how you guys doing? To what do I owe this pleasure?"

They began speaking in unison. "Ms. Lucy, it's time that you know the truth."

"The truth?" Just when you think the coast is clear here comes a tidal wave. Could it be that these men are here to come clean about what happened to the three? What the hell do they know?

Again with the unison speaking. "Yes, ma'am, the truth."

"Listen, I'm going to need just one of you to speak, excuse me but this echo shit is starting to scare me. And if you're here to quit and feel uneasy, I understand. I have to get to the airport in a few minutes but again don't worry about my feelings. I can fully understand your need to no longer work at the foundation. Believe me you, I've considered such the reality."

"We're getting married, Ms. Lucy. And we'd like for you to sing at our ceremony. When I heard your voice back there at the funeral I told Riley that we need you to sing for the union of our love."

I sat there looking dumbfounded and amazed at what my ears witnessed. Glory be to God, they weren't interested in quitting on me. I seriously can't afford to lose any more good workers. But how do you like those apples? Two highly attractive men never even hit the market. The thought never crossed my mind that they were gay, would have sworn my life away on a stack of Bibles that they were both married to women.

"Guys, I didn't know! But of course, I'd be delighted to sing at your wedding. Oh my God. this is great news. I thought you two were getting ready to quit."

"No no, we love this place," said Theodore with Riley shaking his head in agreement.

"I don't mind helping you two out in any way possible. If I can do more, please let me know. But listen, I need help and you two fit the bill. My best friend's husband has had a stroke and I need to get away to Seattle for a week or two. Actually, I need to be packing right now. Would you two be willing to man the office for me? You wouldn't have to do anything major but continue to be the face of the foundation. I can handle the bulk of the paperwork from my laptop."

Again they responded like Siamese twins. "Yes, we got your back." The rest was history. We walked and talked over everything that my traveling mind could think of while I got my things packed. As my cousin Faith would say "Look at God!". Another way was made out of no way. Before long Jayden joined us. We said our goodbyes and on my way to the airport I was confident all would be well. My soul had peace with my decision. I boarded my flight just knowing all would be well. Looking back in the distance I saw the man of my reality smiling and blowing kisses in my direction. What on earth did I do to deserve such love?

After I took my seat thoughts immediately went to Buck. My big cuddle bear has had a stroke. A stroke is just crazy, this man runs five miles a day and always eats cleaner than clean. It just goes to show that in a moment's notice the light can flicker from your eyes and there's not a damn thing you can do about it but accept the call. I closed my eyes and reclined my head back while focusing every healing vibe of my soul to my dear friend. Only if these four hours would just melt away to dust. Being available when called makes all the difference in the world.

The moment my flight landed I hopped in a renter and hauled it straight to the hospital. I knew Shelia would be there by his side but deep down I felt like I was the key to his survival. At least I hoped I would be. One thing about Seattle, once you've learned your way around town you never really forget, the roads may change but the path remains the same. She had left a message that I missed during the flight telling me to call and she'd pick me up but I didn't bother calling. The only thing I needed was the hospital name again. I couldn't remember if she said Seattle Grace or Mercy Grace Hospital but then it hit me Seattle Grace is just for mental patients. How could I ever forget the place my uncle had me confined after the attack? I wouldn't describe myself as mentally torn but deep down something other than my virginity had broken within. In fact, it was here there that I first met Buck. He was a young green attendee at the time but at the same time so knowledgeable and compassionate. Lord Jesus, help my friend.

At the first sighting of the hospital a strange chill went coursing through my veins. That feeling stuck with me from the parking deck to the check-in window, the elevator ride up to the 8th floor and until I walked into room 821. There he lay strapped to all those machines taking in those deep ghastly sounding breaths. While the machines were doing their jobs and making noise. I looked upon my gentle giant and thought back on the many times he came through for me even before there was Shelia, and it made me weep. All those years ago when he wanted to marry me came flushing to the forefront. I wanted to keep things like they were, keep us as friends. He was the first and only father figure that Remi ever knew. Now if not by the grace of God he won't be around too much longer. He doesn't even know that I am here in the room. But at the slightest possibility that he knows that I am here I stood to the corner of the room and got my crying out before I walked to his bedside and held his soft hand. I need to say something just for the sake of saying something.

"Larry Buckner, what have you gotten yourself into? I'm going to need you to get up and start moving around. You were supposed to be in Texas this weekend, did you forget our deal homie?"

Still he lay quiet and motionless in a state of existence I've not ever known him to mimic. I missed that voice and that squeaky laugh. I started to talk again this time while grasping both his hands.

"Larry, it's Lucy and I know you can hear me. Please don't die on me. You're one of my best friends. I just can't bear to lose another rock from my foundation. We need you here. I know that light might be bright but dammit turn it down, you got lots more living to do down here. You can fight this thing, it's not your time…" My voice cracked and he gripped both my hands tight and quick. Being optimistic and so hopeful I took this as a sign of life. After all, not all sickness is unto death. All of this happened in split seconds of time. The next thing I heard, "Mommy!". My baby had found me. I didn't want him to see nor know that I had been crying so I wiped my eyes quickly and greeted my little king with hugs and kisses. He hugged his mommy's neck so tight I just knew I'd pass out if he didn't release.

"There's my big man. Look how big you've grown. Where's you're TT, Shelia?"

"She's outside with the doctor."

When we walked to the door I saw Shelia but I also saw the face of the doctor. It'd been upwards to fifteen years since that night but his face remains fresh to my sight. I really couldn't believe my eyes. It really felt like life was throwing fastballs at me quicker than I can bat. They say this is a small world but got-damn I'm starting to believe small is the understatement. I quickly snatched us back into the room while trying to compose myself for the inevitable, if and when he enters the room. Hopefully he won't recognize me. I took a seat in the corner towards the window.

When I looked into my big man's face I saw what I never had once tried to see. The resemblance of the doctor and Remi all became clear. Like a crystal. I smiled and listened to my Remi tell me all about his adventures while a single tear dropped from my left eye. 'God, if you can hear me take me now, Lord,' was my spirit's cry, right where I sit. It just doesn't make no sense. I'm catching hell at my home, hell with holding on to my friends, now I get the hell in knowing and seeing Remi's real father…Dr. Samuel Teats. The man who had a part in raping me. What really puzzles me is this….he's supposed to have been purged from this earth.

The moment I discovered and catastrophically realized what happened, I called Uncle Jack. He and his crew came to campus and took care of the problem. On that same day he swept me from my campus and I never looked back. I left that life, tossed my identity and put Southern California far in the rearview mirror. The view was so far that everything appeared small. I never once questioned him on what happened but I assumed the boys were dead. Hell, he said they'd never know life again. To me that meant they'd been swept from the face of this earth. Not until today had I ever considered otherwise.

It wasn't long before Shelia entered the room. She didn't look herself at all. Naturally, considering all things to be so dismally unequal. Again, very understandable with her situation. I just reached out for my dear friend and said nothing. Her pain filled the room. Little Remi embraced us and told Shelia, "TT Shelia, Uncle Buck said to be strong." Within seconds of him saying that, the machines went crazy beeping and the nurses and doctors came rushing in to try to revive our flatlining love. His death was called at 5:15 p.m. Shelia just stood there at the foot of the bed gazing upon him saying nothing.

I searched my mind over far and near for the right thing to say but I had no words. What do you say to the woman who just lost the love of her life? You say nothing. You do nothing. I just kept quiet and waited. She and Buck had kept the only child they ever knew all summer. Unfortunately, there was no little Shelia or Buck to recount time on. My friend has beautiful bright blue eyes, but they are now a dulling gray. She stood there at his lifeless feet for greater than 30 minutes quiet and motionless before our silence was broken by the doctor. Not once did he look in my direction and remember my face. I was a bit disappointed even though I didn't really want to relive that forgotten yesterday. I decided it was best to allow this giant to stay buried. I wonder if he even looked at Remi and thought okay this kid looks familiar.

Shelia finally broke her silence.

"I'm coming back to Texas with you. I can't live here alone without Buck. Not no time soon."

"Sure, you can come with me. We'll discuss this after we get all the funeral plans arranged."

"There won't be a funeral. He wouldn't hear of it."

It grew increasingly hard to walk around the house without even a hint of Buck's spirit. It was even harder seeing Shelia paralyzed in her shoes and I could do nothing but pray. She didn't speak much but by the third night she came to the room after I had put Remi down for the night, just stood at the door like a zombie. I lay there looking into her eyes as a smile began to form. We smiled at each other. She hadn't said a word or even appeared human since the hospital. But of course, when she did decide to speak her focus was on me and not of herself.

"Lucy, what did you think when you saw him?"

"I just didn't want him to die too, Shelia. I stood there and spoke to him like I normally would but he wouldn't respond to me."

"No, not Buck, Lucy, the Doctor. I saw Remi all over his face when he first entered Buck's room. But when he told me where and when he went undergrad, it became clear that he was your guy."

Tears flowed down my face at first thought of Buck but then I began to weep over my own situation. I thought I'd try to forget the whole ordeal but of course she would notice. It all came on me like a violent wind.

"Shelia, I really want to be angry with him and see him suffer."

"But you really feel otherwise?"

"Yes. I haven't told you but in my city I've been catching hell. I have some great friends there but I'm also working against some kind of invisible mob. This group steals the dreams of the people and turns right around and kills them after they've toyed them around enough. Three of my staff members were murdered in an old mine and on the same night they were hit by a train."

She started to laugh.

"Girl, what the hell you been reading? You'd say anything to cheer me up. That's why you my girl."

"No, Shelia, I'm serious, there is some crazy shit going on in Schuster and I aim to get to the bottom of it all. Also, just so you know there's a hit on the lives of those close to me. I need you to be sure you want to go home with me."

"You're really serious, aren't you?"

"Deadass."

"So, you had all this action going on down there and never even said a word? You knew we'd be there in a heartbeat. Okay, what are we going to do about Doctor Rape-a-Hoe?"

"Just leave him be. I know all I need to know for now. He'll see me when it's time."

"Look at you sounding all Godfather-ish!!!".

We sat there laughing and crying. While it seemed like a lifetime had passed since I'd heard joy. I know the road is long with many miles to her recovery but she's going to make it. Actually, we're going to be better than alright.

"Girl, I didn't think I could smile without him. I never wanted to find out either. You know the last thing he told me before the heart attack was you got to start stepping out more."

"What was all of that about? You lived a life independent of him, right?"

"Kinda sorta no. I don't know when it happened but somehow I stopped leaving his side. In the last couple of years it's like I had some deep sixth sense that was expecting this day to come. I just felt the need to spend every possible moment with him. Now that the day has come and gone. I'm almost at peace with the situation. Though I keep wanting to wake up from this terrible dream. I'm not going to do anything but make myself crazy here alone so I'm coming with you. Suicide mission or not. You my girl and I'm with you no matter what. I'm bringing my seventeen brothers and their friends, so we got nothing to worry about. I got five more on standby. But let's hear this story from the very top. It sounds like we're going to need lots of wine."

We sat in the kitchen sipping on wine glass refills one after another while I rehashed the experience from Little Raphael to the Big Slim's funeral. It all felt like old times until she started to cry again. Even then I just reached across the table and held my friend's hand. Assurance came from my hands and flowed to her spirit. Sometimes no words are the best words. After a while we started back laughing and talking and soon went to sleep on the sofa like the old days. Only Buck won't be waking us with chocolate chip pancakes and bacon. I can't be sure if I ever attempted to travel to dreamland. It seemed to me I was close to boarding the bus when my cell began to ring profusely. Indeed, I'm surprised it didn't wake Shelia but with the amount of wine she drank she could easily sleep through the Apocalypse. It was Jayden on the other side of the line. What he said didn't make sense the first two times but before he could repeat the third time it all made sense. Or I should say it became clear. I started a war and now the wolves have come out of the high country to devour the sheep.

Sitting there watching the sunrise is still one of the most serene moments of the day. The sun makes no fuss over where you see her rise. One thing remains constant, she's going to rise through the mightiest of dark nights without a fight. I had been sitting on the balcony wide awake since his call. Listening to the various voicemails from the workers and volunteers only pissed me off even more. I knew everyone was concerned but I just didn't need any more sorry's. Sorry just doesn't fix it. Then there was a text from an unknown number with pictures of the ruins and a picture of the gold foil envelope with 'he's been here' written on it. Not once did I consider this could be some kind of electrical wiring issue. I knew he was involved. I called the number but only got a message saying the number was no longer in service. Must have been a burner. There I stood on the balcony trying to convince myself that going back to Schuster was a good idea. I even tried to convince myself into believing I could just forget that place and never return. After all the hell I've endured quitting seems like a perfect option. On top of this sordid mess I saw who I knew without a shadow of doubt was Remi's father today and he never knew it was me. I wonder if he even noticed Remi favored him so greatly. Google told of his careers and great accomplishments. They talk him up like he's an innocent lamb without a spot or blemish, a true Saint. These feelings I was feeling made me know I hadn't filed this experience in the sea of forgotten nightmares. The pressure of it all was starting to roll in with the tide the past was seeping back into my vision quickly.

Some things from the past have to be confronted before they can be properly resolved. Go figure Remi has a celebrated surgeon and equally successful entrepreneur for a father and the man happens to be a rapist. Talk about tough-ass luck. It was time to call him. The very fact that I'm scrolling through my contact list for his number and knowing the number is still in rotation speaks volumes for the universe. My attitude is in a mood that says forget how it turns out. It's either do or don't. When I finally saw his name I hit the call button with all give a damns left to fall as they may. The phone rang twice and he answered almost instantly.

"Hello my niece."

"Jack, I thought you took care of it. You told me you took care of the situation. But yet yesterday I saw him. He's gone on to have a very successful career in medicine. With no remembrance of his sin. Help me understand why you lied to me. Just why did you lie?"

"Marie, he's the only one alive. I…"

"It's Lucy now and I don't care if he's the only one alive."

"Okay, Ms. Lucy, I'm sorry but if you didn't care then why in the hell have you called today at 5:53 a.m. in the damn morning? You haven't spoken to me since this incident. You changed your name, created a new life for yourself and moved to that delightful little town trying to save the world. All the while sinking down in your own pity."

"You're right, I don't know why I called you today. Just the sight of knowing he's doing well and I'm living with the open wound and constantly watching over my back just doesn't sit well with me."

"For small consolation it as it appears. Ms. Lucy, he watched a masked man slaughter his two friends right in front of him all the while begging to know why they were losing their lives only to hear "atonement for sin" over and over again until they drew in their last breath. Even more so he was left in a cage for a month and fed the minimum to keep death away. He rose, slept, and ate in the wallow of his own filth and when he imagined life couldn't get any worse,. I released him with a guarantee of death if he ever so much as breathed on that moment. So yeah, baby girl, he might have forgotten your beautiful face or even your tearful screams,

133

but he'll never forget to do the right thing again. And I remind him every year with pictures of himself in that pit with the rotting corpse of his friends. So consider the debt paid and move on with your life. But let's be real, this is not why you called me. It's only a symptom of the sickness."

I ended the call expecting that he'd call back but when he didn't I wasn't all too surprised. There was a need to lay it all out on the table but my pride got thick and fear overtook my thoughts. I never knew the full extent of his reach but it stretched far enough that I grew to fear him. I don't know but I think I can handle this on my own. I have enough blood on my hands already that I didn't work for, this time I'll do the tree chopping and no matter what this tree will fall from my efforts.

I deleted his name from my contacts and cleared the call log to make sure I wouldn't call back. As crazy as it sounds I felt a bit lighter. Maybe some weight was lifted from my heart. What started as a bright shiny day had soon turned to just another day with light. In going back into the house I looked in on everyone. Remi was still fast asleep clutching his animal friend and Shelia was now nearly off the sofa. If anything was gained from this call it was to maybe leave the past where it dwells and do my damnedest to make this present madness a past experience.

But why do I feel like I should be terribly upset and depressed? Here I sat in the kitchen eating some kind of sweet cereal almost content. The situation ain't good but way down on the inside I know it will be alright. My main concern is the children. The building is just a building but it's the children that make the foundation and I need a place for them to continue forward. Ironically, sugar is said to make you get all scatterbrained but this bowl was giving me life.

"I got it!"

"You got what, Mommy?" Lost in my own thoughts I didn't see nor hear Remi come pull up a seat for his bowl.

"Oh, hey there, Mommy's big man. I was thinking about where I could house the children for the foundation. And the place was right in plain sight. The gymnasium next door will be perfect."

"I want pancakes and bacon."

Talk about falling from the apple tree. I was just not too long ago thinking about Buck's pancakes. He's been here all summer with the gentle giant catering to his taste buds' desire.

"No problem, buddy, pancakes and bacon coming right up. Go see if Big Shelia is up for breakfast."

"Big Shelia! That's Aunt Shelia in there."

"It's an old nickname, just say it to her, it'll make her happy."

He scurried across the hallway to the living room. I didn't hear him say it but I heard Shelia holler and laughing like a hyena. It's funny how the mind works. You don't think about a particular thing for years then all of a sudden it shows up when you need it but least expect it. Some real Nanny McPhee shit.

About fifteen minutes she and Remi returned looking refreshed and dressed for the breakfast feast.

"I see you're still the breakfast queen."

"Yes yes you know, Buh...", I figured it had to be too soon to even say his name.

"Girl, don't worry about it. I'm going to have my moments whether he's mentioned or not. You good, I'm good, Remi's good....We All Good!. Let's eat these pancakes!"

My friend who had just lost her right leg and is now otherwise considered a cripple just smiled and said it's going to be all good. Buck's gift of peace definitely rubbed off on anyone who took the time to let him minister to their life. He was one of the best damn counselors I'll ever know. Our beginning, and the ending was at a hospital. It's understood that God Almighty has a plan but it's in times like these that I wonder about this plan's worth.

"Girl, stop ya daydreaming and pass that bacon this way, Gah." Remi giggled in her direction.

Sitting there at the table watching them eat and joke around felt familiar yet odd. This void is understandable but occurring a bit too often. I hadn't the chance to mourn Big Slim and now Buck's gone. In my mind's ear I can hear Marcelle recite just as loud "all will crumble around you." It was like he was a warlock or some other side of madness. But this can't get me down too low. In the midst of all this regret, I missed several calls and messages from Jayden.

Yes, I needed to return the calls but all of that could wait. What the hell else could happen? The million-dollar question that should never be asked. One of the texts read: 'They have found two burned bodies in a closet of the foundation.' If that wasn't enough the next message just about knocked me to the floor: 'they've taken Lyles in for questioning and then charged him with murder and arson, there is no option for bail. They claim to have a witness who saw Lyles going inside the building with a big gas jug. I know you're in a situation but please call me back. I need to hear your voice.'

Sadness rained down over my body but then came rage. Before I knew it I was calling Marcelle; the call went straight to voicemail.

"It's bad enough that you burned my building but now you're picking with my people. You sick son of a bitch know this! When I mow the grass, I spray the weeds. Go ahead and laugh now but I'll have the last laugh." The voicemail tone beeped, then the call disconnected.

Standing there in the shower I nearly collapsed from all the tears. Somehow, I mustered the strength to whisper a prayer, "God. I know You hear me always. Lord, I need You to fight this battle. Help us take a stand, Father," I don't pray all that much, but Mom always told me when you get slack on God, He knows how to let your course bring you back to Him. Indeed, I haven't given Him much of my time over the years. I let what happened to me all of those years make me turn my back on His comfort. Not to say I stopped believing but more or less I stopped trusting His judgment. Disbelief is one of the enemy's biggest plots for destruction. The things that happen down here in this life are mere moves of consequence but rarely is the case coincidental. Mom would often reassure me with this chant, "All things work together for the good of they that love the Lord and are called according to His purposes." I love the Lord and despite my absence I still believe I'm called according to His purpose. Marcelle, this order or whatever the hell can't win this fight. I got an army of angels all around me and mine. We will be good.

Once I got myself cleaned and together I found the family outside on the balcony.

"Washed all that sin off , huh? I'mma need you to pay that water bill. We don't do no 30-minute showers around here, gah. This ain't the Hilton. But for real how you feeling? You looked like something else was up earlier."

"The foundation burned and there were two bodies found inside."

My gut's reaction was to board a plane and get home ASAP but then the need subsided. Lyles left a message that couldn't have been more than 15 seconds long. "Find your peace, Lucy All is well."

Though the words were few the message was clear. He was short on time but he knew just what to say to ease my tensions. In fact, his words gave me the strength to decide to go back to my parents' home. No moment in life is coincidental, this would be a chance to create some good memories with my son and Big Shelia. It's finally time to close the door on the past. Accepting my limitations and shortcomings is the foundation for my healing and advancement. Closure does the spirit good. After all, life is short and all around me its fleeting daily, in the blink of an eye it could be called to its end. I'm sure the drive back home will be tense but I can do it. This day never crossed my mind because I never intended to plan it but it's time to go home and make peace with the pain. They needed to see where I came from, I needed to get past the pain of looking back. So we packed Shelia's car and off we went to Sunnyside South Central, Los Angeles. Upon arriving at 1616 South Normandie Ave., the place I stopped calling home for upwards of 17 years ,the amazement in Remi's eyes and the shock on Shelia's face could have bought several mansions. The house is a miniature replica of the White House.

"Welcome to my parents' house…the White House."

"You never said you were the First Child of America. How about this, Lucy is the President's kid. Remi, you want to go explore the Oval Office?"

"Always the smartass. Here's the key, go on your voyage. I'll just fight with the luggage all by my lonesome."

"Come on, Remi, let's help your mommy first then we'll have some real fun."

"Okay, Big Shelia, but let's move fast!"

I could have fainted from laughing. Shelia just stood turning all red face trying to contain her laugh but it burst through like a pricked balloon.

She mouthed in my direction, "I'm kicking your ass, just you wait." I only laughed that much harder and could only give her two thumbs up.

It's amazing how even the smallest memory has a way of impressing itself on you like a catastrophic event when the moment is right. While standing there grazing on the moment I remembered how when friends would come over my dad always told the story of he came about owning the house. He'd say, "We were driving down the road letting the air blow the beach sand from our bodies and out the clear blue Lucinda starts screaming like a banshee, 'that's the White House. That's the house. That's our home! Pullover, Paul, I got to have this house.'" Had it not been for sale my mom would have sweet-talked the owners into to making the sale happen.

"Wow, Mommy, you lived in the White House, was my Pawpaw the President?"

"No, not the President, but he was just as powerful in my sight. This house was just built to look like the White House, it is what they call it a replica. My dad's office was even patterned after the Oval Office."

"No one lives here now, Lucy?"

"No, I haven't had a renter in about a year."

"You rent this place out? Wow, never even knew it existed."

"Yeah, my Uncle Jack has been the caregiver since my parents went away. But, umm, let's get this stuff inside so I can give you two a tour of the place and we can get settled inside."

They walked ahead, while the old memories of that night paralyzed me at the gate's entrance. The air got too thick to breathe while my whole being started saying "you're not ready for this" but then I felt Remi tugging at my hand and looked up to the porch and saw Shelia's smile pressing through her disguised pain. All this time I thought walking away from this place meant that I survived pain somehow. When you walk far enough away from something it's easier to think you're healed or to put it behind you when in all actuality you're just running away. To truly overcome you have to face the devil face to face and just start kicking his ass like you know your life matters. After all these years upon opening the door I can still smell the sweet fragrance of my mom's perfume infused all over the place. Again familiar places have that effect on the brain. A psychologist once told me sometimes you can smell a memory, in some cases you can even taste it. Remi took off like the Roadrunner tracing from room to room. While Shelia taking note of my hesitations, locked her arm into my mine for encouragement.

"I'm right here, just hold it tight and keep it loose. It's gonna be alright, I know this feeling."

I had shared many things with her and Buck but I never told them about what really happened here on my seventeenth birthday. In fact, I never thought I would ever have to, it's normal for folks to have lost their parents and that's what I persuaded everyone to think. I received empathy but definitely not the amount of pity and fragility of knowing one's parents were murdered in their living room on your birthday which so happens to be prom night. The omittance of such fact was my outlet, then when the rape occurred it just overwrote the situation with something almost equally shittier. Turning to make sure the black metal storm screen door was secured I suddenly felt inspired.

"I'm good, Big Shelia, let's go find Remi and go upstairs to the attic, there are some things I want you two to see."

"Alright, that's my girl. But what we gonna do for food? Cause I am starved."

"Girl, this ain't rainy Seattle, this is South Central Los Angeles. We ordering take out, because I like living, these gangstas don't know me no more. As a matter of fact, let's go get the rest of the bags out of the car before it gets dark." She laughed hard. "But, Shelia, I'm for real, let's get the bags!"

We were nearly back in the house when I heard my name. "YooHoo, Marie Antionette! Child, is that you?"

I hadn't heard her voice in what seemed like ages but that signature YooHoo would stand out in the midst of a thousand. Ms. Nita Durby was always great to my family and me. The woman has to be about a hundred years old and I'm willing to bet she's still driving these streets jumping on the sidewalks scaring the hell out of people.

"Miss Durby! Yes, ma'am, it's me."

"Child, y'all better get on over here and have some of this food."

"Girl, can she cook?" Food was all Shelia needed to hear.

"Short answer, she from Mississippi."

"You ain't said nothing but a word, go get yo baby, I'm headed to Ms. Mississippi's house."

Well no need for takeout, dinner has been solved! Downhome cooking to the rescue.

Both Ms. Nita and Shelia never knew a stranger they didn't call friend. Dinner was just as I remember and even better. Out of all these years this woman is still rendering up meals befitting the royals. My folks really enjoyed her company. Aunt Nita's niece Felecia and her children came over from next door. She and I were about maybe a year or two apart in age but were pretty good friends back in the day. Her two boys were well mannered. Remi was ecstatic to have other children around. He quickly left our sides to take on their company. Though I hadn't seen these folks in upwards of many years I still felt connected. So much so that I allowed Remi to follow them over to their home alone but full belly Shelia tagged along. The quiet moment allowed room for Ms. Nita to start her inquiries.

"Little Marie, I always expected you to return home for a visit. But it was looking like such an expectation was never nearing fruition. But I sure am glad to see you. Looking just as beautiful as your dear mother. So child, tell me what's really been going on in your life. Give me the short read as you young folks say."

"I never thought I would come back here, Ms. Nita. Uncle Jack said it wasn't safe here anymore for me. You know I still don't know all the specifics of what really happened to my parents. Their deaths are still a mystery to me."

"What made you think things had changed my dear?"

"Well you're here after all these years. Ms. Nita, as I look back on life I notice that I have just been swapping out from one bad situation to the next and in just about all things I have been running. I won't run anymore. What's for me will indeed come and I shall be ready."

"Baby, I understand. I left Mississippi and a no-good husband there in the midnight hour and didn't look back. When that bastard found me out here I was ready for him.

He forced his way into this house and I played the role of the battered wife for a quick minute until I reached my six sisters. Chile, I popped a cap in his ass that was heard around the nation." You talk about some funny stories. This woman had a bag full. I laughed for what seemed like hours.

Indeed, it's great to know that after many years I can still sit and have a good laugh with an old friend. No weird factor involved. I could have just talked to her for days, her wisdom and character just enveloped my spirit. She reminded me so much of Big Slim, in fact they could have been sisters. It wasn't long before Shelia came back with Remi draped over her left shoulder. The little tyke had played out. Ms. Nita helped me gather our things and bagged a couple of to-go plates just in case the hunger struck again. We said our goodbyes and journeyed back across the street. She stood there in the door of her porch waiting patiently for us to make it home safely. I didn't notice until I turned to flip down the deadbolt on the door, when I saw her waving in my direction.

Once back in the house Shelia went from room to room with Remi before she came back with a look of confusion on her face.

"Umm, sister, you didn't say we were gonna be camping out on the floor. Hell, I could have brought my air mattress. I'm a little too old to be playing a slumber party. What we gonna do?"

I sighed softly and chuckled. "Girl, give me my baby, you got his head dangling like a rag doll. Have a little faith in ya girl and follow me upstairs to the attic."

"Sister, is that where y'all keep all the furniture? I ain't trying to be looking at no home videos or old pictures tonight. I need a shower and a nap."

When this child gets sleepy she gets anal.

"Just follow me, Sister."

"You can go on somewhere else with that Sista shit. Now, I'm ready to sleep. Ain't got time to be walking all over this big ass house."

From the outside you wouldn't know it but the house has a full attic that can easily double as a full apartment floor. Well it's kind of sealed off from the regular eye. Shelia's frustration wore no mask. You could even hear it in her walk. Those size 8's were stomping the hell out the floor. Finally we entered the third bedroom on the second floor and I said, "we've almost arrived." Turned and locked the doorknob. Shelia stood there in the empty room about to full-on snap out. Before she could do it I opened the closet door and went directly to the back. I pressed the latch on the inner side of the wall shelf and gained access to the stairway that led to the attic. It was some real Harry Potter wizard work but my parents had the upstairs restructured for this very purpose. Why they did this I'll never know. Once we were inside I closed the door and ushered her up the stairs. I was pleasantly surprised to find the area laid out perfectly as I needed it to be. Family pictures were on the walls, all the important keepsakes were in place to comfort my soul. The attic has two bedrooms and two baths, a full kitchen, a living room area and one office area. Everything looked like home. After doing a quick scan of everything she looked in my direction and asked, "Just the who the hell were your parents? What did they do for a living? My God, Lucy, you didn't tell us a lot. I expect a debriefing on tomorrow, SISTA. But hell we did all this traveling in this house and forgot our things downstairs."

"Girl, I don't even know where to begin. But no worries, I got that covered already. There's a service elevator to your right in that back wall. Just hit the button on the wall. I put our bags inside already."

"When did you have time to do that?"

"My goodness aren't you the little question bee. Just press the button, girl. I'm going to put Remi to bed."

"Don't do me like that, you the one that lived in damn McGyver's house. I'm just trying to get an understanding."

Understanding, now that's something I still lack. Tucking my little man in my childhood bed brought back the many memories of my mom doing this very same thing to me every night until I thought I was too big for her snuggie tuggies. The child was dead asleep but he whispered, "I love you, Mommy," and disappeared into the dream world. My heart bubbled over with the joy of the world spilling out. When I came back to help Shelia I found her sitting on the sofa reading something. She looked up in my direction all teary-eyed. Must have been a Buck moment. I don't know how she managed to go on this long but she's held up solidly well. I sat there beside her and just held her hand. Saying nothing vocally but allowing my heart to carry the moment.

"Lucy, thank you for bringing me along. You might not understand this but I'm so alone. My baby is gone and he ain't coming back no more." She began to cry softly to herself.

This was the time to console her with some soul-soothing words but I had nothing that would even scratch the surface of her pain and brighten her mood. Instead I dimmed the lights and turned my attention to look out the porthole window. Nothing particular caught my attention but the front gate. To be honest I have no idea why I began to speak but this felt like the right time to lay it all out on the line.

"You know, Shelia, they say it gets easier with time. But they lied. You can run from it but you can never hide from it. It always has a way of catching up to you,

145

sometimes the grip is loose but for the most part it's tighter than hell's gate. Many years ago I left home for the prom with no date but my girl Felicia across street that rode with me. My parents and Ms. Nita took all sorts of pictures downstairs in the living room. Everyone was so super happy. We were soon to be going off to college and start our next life. My dress was a blue ballroom gown and hers was an equally nice silver dress. We should have had dates as beautiful as we looked. The parents had just bought me an Audi Coupe in black; man, I loved that car once I learned to shift the gears properly. Dad made sure I knew how to stick that thang just right. Our prom theme for the evening was make it last forever, believe me you it was a moment straight out the hands of a dream. We danced, we laughed, and we cried because I guess we all understood that the end was near. One of the last songs to be played that night was "Graduation" by Vitamin C. Man, why did they play that song? Even the football players were in tears. At the close of the evening the class took our final group photo. Everyone was supposed to be meet up in the Hills for the afterparty at Parker Rodgers' uncle's house. I had forgotten to bring my bag with the change of clothes but Felicia was good. She was going to ride back home with me but I told her to go ahead, that I'd meet them there. Only I never caught up with them that night. I could see the police and ambulance lights from Western Avenue. Nothing unusual for Los Angeles, I remember thinking Oh God what has happened now. As I got closer I could see the crowd was at my house. Even then I thought someone got shot at the bus stop in front of the house. I was ready to hear my dad's spin on the story. I parked down the street from the house and walked to the property. To this day I have no clue where Ms. Nita came from but I heard her scream, 'My Marie Chile, Jesus help us, Lord!' I froze right there as she and an officer approached the gate entrance. It was then that I knew something was terribly wrong. Ms. Nita was there holding my hand and speaking but I don't remember understanding her words. From the gate I saw their bodies on the floor covered with white sheets drenched in their red blood. I must have blacked out because when I woke up I was in the hospital with Uncle Jack sitting adjacent to my bed watching me like a hawk. I wanted to scream like my body was racked with pain but instead I laid there just like you are today and just cried softly. There would be no one words that could appease me for the months to come. I lived with Uncle Jack in San Jose until it was time for me to start college. He just knew that I'd lost my interest, in fact I felt the same until it was time. The day before I needed to check in for the summer session it was like I was released from what was holding me. Suddenly I was with this need to get away. Get away I did, I started college there at Chapman University in Orange, California. Everything actually went better than well for those first two years. Then just as I had begun to think my life had sustained all the horrors of this world it would ever need to withstand, it happened. I got popped upside the head leaving the library and was taken to some basement and raped by four or five young men. Remi's father the good doctor just so happened to have been the last to take my once virgin lady part for a test ride only unlike the others his deposit stuck. Until now I never knew who the father of my child could be. I remember the painful sex and the voices and laughter but my vision was always hazy on the faces of the men that night."

I never once looked back to see if she were awake or no. Really it didn't matter if she were awake or sleep. My heart needed to dump this load to the atmosphere some way somehow. I wouldn't need to tell this story again for at least 10 or 12 more years from now. But even then it'll be in the form of a letter. I just can't phantom the idea of speaking this into the ears of my son. When the time is right my child will read this sordid past of his mother and somehow love me even more than his yesterday. Gazing out that window did nothing for my spirits. It only helped me to see the real picture. Those nights were nothing less than bad moments but still nothing more than yesterday's reality. From the refection of the window I could see my friend's body was indeed stretched out on the couch. It was finally off my chest so I stood there quietly watching the cars kill themselves trying to beat the yellow street light.

"Sista, you thought I was sleep didn't ya? Girl, I heard ever word. Know this, you are the epitome of a diamond in the rough. Nothing this side of Hell can ever contain you. Please know that you've given me strength to push. Buck once tried to share your story with me but I refused. Something just never felt right hearing it from him and not you. I never wanted to have you recount that past life but I always knew this moment would one day get here. If you don't believe in your will to live, look at your little one. Here you are his mother that's HIV Positive and you had a full-term natural birth baby who has no hints of the condition. Tell me God ain't Real. But, girl, come on let's get this sleep."

It was that point of the night when traffic had diminished away. The moon sat high in the sky in a way that caused my reflection to mirror my making. She stood there beside me holding my hand while we both gazed out the window into the deep of the night each tearing up for reasons of our own accord. I whispered, "I don't know if we're safe here. I want to leave here tomorrow and never look back. My home is over 2,000 miles east. You get some rest, I'm going to pack up the photos and a few other remembrances of my folks and I'll be off to bed shortly."

"Lucy, if safety was a measure to you then why the hell are we even here? I didn't come all this way to die. If I wasn't so beat I'd say let's get the hell out of here tonight but I believe we can manage. But before I do all that is there a way to prevent that service elevator from moving tonight? What about that hideaway staircase, is it secure?"

She posed the big picture questions. But I had the bases covered already. The elevator was wedged to prevent its calling and the staircase door was locked and secured with the steel bar that sat in two steel like handles that would stop the door from being forced open. After creating this alarm I found it difficult to silence its effect on her. "I don't like this not one bit, Lucy. I should have known something was up when I looked around this whole damn house and saw nothing but empty rooms and then we get up here and it's like damn Fort Knox lockdown mode. But don't get me wrong, Sis, I'm not mad or anything but I just hate to be blindsided. You obviously knew the risk of being here and I know I said I'm here for it all but gotdamn let me know what's up. But everything is fine, right? We are safe to make it through the night?"

"Yes, everything is fine, Shelia. I'm sorry."

"No need to be sorry. Let's just… as of matter fact don't even think more of it. I'm tired and starting to over react. Let's get some rest and I'll help you pack in the morning. Night."

"Night."

She went to bed while I continued to stand there at the window feeling like a big blob of nothing. She was right, I did know the possible risk and never thought twice of involving her or my Remi for that matter. I really should be ashamed of myself. While I stood there beating myself up I saw Ms. Nita come out, step out her front door to the stoop where she stood for a quick minute until this blacked out Suburban pulled up and I saw her point in this direction. The car did a quick heavy U-turn and shot past the house. My heart began to pulsate like a bass drum. Back in the day folks said that she was a big time drug dealer. I knew the rumors but I could never see her as a gangster lady. She was sweet but very firm. Knowing what I presently understand we can't put anything beneath any one person. It's second nature for me to correlate that black Suburban with the likes of the black Tahoe from Schuster.

My being wanted to enter panic mood but in glancing at the TV I remembered the surveillance system on setting two. The coast appeared clear, no army of robbers were waiting to bum rush the place. There simply is no need to worry . I'm over 2,000 miles away from my troubles. I just need to rest, everything gets clearer after resting. Before going to bed I did a walkthrough like my mother did every night no matter how she felt. Sometimes I'd wake up to her presence either standing at the door watching me sleep or just as she'd be closing the door. A deaf man could hear Shelia snoring, but my Remi just lay there sleeping soundly safe in the hands of his dreams. After standing there for a while taking in his beauty I joined him there in the bed. Just as I got comfortable on my pillow he said it. "Good night, Mommy, all will be well." His small nuggets of sleepy faith put my soul at complete ease and I rested.

For these last few months sleeping has been a real chore. Most nights I lay in bed thinking on the what ifs and maybes of life until I slumber off. Then if there is the slightest noise I'm back awake wondering if my reaper is near. It really is the small things in life that really help us to appreciate this time we have allotted to us. Even still, time really flew by on me, I'm rested but could use a few more hours of shut eye. Everything felt right until I rolled over to the bed empty of Remi. The covers dropped to the floor like heavy rain from heaven. Panic filled my soul. All sorts of wild thoughts rushed through my mind but the worst of it died upon me snatching the bedroom door open. He and Shelia stood in the kitchen stirring up breakfast. They didn't see my face or else they'd saw the despair that covered it. I eased the door shut and silently cried like a baby as I eased to the floor using my body to jam the door and prevent entry.

150

This life is really getting to my head. Living in constant fear of some damn invisible killer just isn't right. The storms of life just aren't rolling past my front door as they should. There won't be any rest until all of this madness has come to an end. So I sat there and dried my tears and whispered a prayer to the Man Upstairs thanking Him for His grace and I asked for strength and protection to see this thing through and over. It would have been nice to have stayed on in town a bit longer but this thing can't be put off any longer. Vacation time we'll have again, this I'm sure. It's now time to go get my peace back. The kingdom suffers violence and that violence takes it by force.

"Hey, Jayden, we're on our way back. We'll be leaving here in the next couple hours. Listen, I know I've been a bit distant these last few weeks and that wasn't fair to you. I can't really explain my actions, all I can say is I'm done with allowing my demons to run amuck in my head. I'm coming to take back what's mine and I'm bringing backup. See you in a day or so."

The voicemail beeped. It's 7:00 something in the morning here and around 10:00 there. He's likely elbow deep in meals from up above. Still, it's sort of strange to get his voicemail. Actually, it's something new to me. I don't think he' s ever not answered my calls on the first try. He'll call back, that I'm sure of.

The smell of breakfast infused the room. Knowing Shelia she pulled out google and found an IHOP or its equivalent. I might be wrong but I could smell the sweet savor of my mother's buttermilk biscuits with a hint of cinnamon. It's amazing how the brain can channel up old smells in familiar places. Here I am in my childhood bed and from the scent of things I'm starting to expect to see my parents waiting outside to hear if I slept well. The reality of knowing that they are no more closer to coming home than the kids of Schuster are to returning to their families made this a sad moment. After all these years I still mourn my family. We never got the closure. I need them here with me but there's not a damn thing I can do to change what's evident. This morning is likely the first time in upwards of 10 or 12 years that I have had a moment but unlike back then I know there's love all around me. So for these small pieces of love I am grateful to get out of bed and face the world or in this case my reality.

"Mommy's up!" my son shouted as he paced around the room like a Tasmanian devil. "Mommy, come sit. Come have breakfast. How did you sleep, Mommy?"

"I slept like a baby with you keeping me safe last night." No lie there. I actually slept like a log because I don't even remember dreaming. "Where'd you guys go to get this tasty smelling breakfast"

"Ms. Nita brought it over. She would have had us over for breakfast but knew we probably needed our rest. So she made a batch of fresh biscuits and rustled up some eggs and bacon and voila we have breakfast."

"Oh, okay, that's wonderful. You guys enjoy and I'll be right back. I need to speak with Aunt Nita real quick." No doubt my perplexed expression said more than my words.

"What's the problem, girl? Are we good?"

"Yeah Yeah, we're good I just need to give her a proper farewell. Y'all eat up and I'll be back in a few and we can start getting ready to hit the road."

She nodded her head like it was understood that everything was clear but by the same token I knew she knew that I was full of shit and at the right time would call me out on it. But for now it was all good. Sure enough we agreed no more secrets and I'm sticking to my word; I just need to clear the air.

Waiting to cross the road after all these years is still a comical feat. The red light is evident and the drivers are gunning their cars just to beat it. In retrospect I remember back to the time when my dad taught me how to cross Norman-Died for the first time. Pops always said be careful crossing Norman-died….cause poor Norman tried but never made to the other side of the road. We are not gonna discuss how petrified that made me of crossing streets. All I can say is, man, I made it. Just as I was about to knock, the screen door was pushed open with laughter. Aunt Nita sat there about to fall from her seat. "Chile, I see you still running like a track star. You crossed that road on four flats like a thoroughbred. Yo daddy still got you thinking about lil Norman. Not that I'm upset to get your company but pray tell the reason for your visit at this hour. Shelia said you all were soon to hit the road after having breakfast. You know even as a little girl you had this terrible poker face. What's on your mind, girl?"

"I saw something from the window last night that concerned me. Now I won't be upset if you tell me the truth."

"The truth you say? The truth about what, chile?"

"To start off I know you know more about my parents than you ever said. Explain their death to me please and then explain that black Suburban you were standing beside last night. Aunt Nita, if you loved me like you say you do and always did lay it all out on the table my dear. I have been through hell on a country mile. I know I can handle the truth."

"Some things can never be uttered without pain accompanying. But yo momma gave me something that I think it's time you read. No think, I know it's time." She stood and turned to open the cedar chest she sat atop of. While she dug around for whatever it was she continued talking. "You know that command station window reflects light from within. For the untrained eye it's just a reflection from the street lights but I know better and you can faintly see the silhouette of a person looking out the window. Before you get to thinking strange it's just a black SUV. It's not the one you've been dreading. The rumors are true. I'm still in the game and believe it or not only death ends my membership. For that bit of knowledge you need to read this." She handed me three basic composition folders secured by two red ribbons. "As for that night. It's a moment of my life that I still have nightmares about. Baby, I had to stand there in that closet and watch that man execute your folks worse than animals at the slaughter. My hands were tied, there was nothing I could do to save them. I tried to get them to take you and run but they said some good would one day come from the pain of their sacrifice. They were tired of covering up wrong with more wrong and they accepted their fates. They told me many things but they never fully explained the wrong. And after the events of that night I never ever wanted to even read the ins and out of their life. Baby, you guard them books better than Moses and the commandments of God. After you've taken it all in, destroy them."

"How'd you get the books?"

"Your momma brought them over the day of your prom. She was so nervous that day I tell ya. I kept telling her just get lost in the wind but she said they couldn't. I was at y'all house after we took all those pictures and that's when a knock was at the door. They stashed me in that service elevator and told me to keep quiet. They tried giving that man the world but he only wanted one thing and all you heard was the slight discharge of his silenced gun and their bodies going thud on the tiled floor. I stood there for about 45 minutes crying and waiting to be sure the coast was clear. Over the years I beat myself up for doing nothing to help them but over time I've come to realize their fates were sealed. When your Uncle Jack got here he collapsed to the floor beside your dad and kept repeating, 'God-Dammit, you knew to call me.' And that's it in a nutshell, baby. The rest you'll have to hear from your momma."

She reached over and wiped my tears. "Now, Chile, if what you going back home to is even similar to your mom's situation, take me with you. I couldn't help your folks, baby, but let me help you. I haven't been to the country in years. It's time for a scenery change." I didn't notice them at first but there laying in the entrance of the main door were two duffle bags. She really was all in. "So what you say, chile, can I tag along on this road to redemption?"

"I don't see no reason why not. I gotta pack up a few things at the house and we'll be on our way. Thanks for the truth, Aunt Nita. But whose gonna handle things while you're away?"

She smiled and opened the security door. "Gal, now don't you go getting in grown folks business. I got this. I'll see you all in an hour or so."

Talk about you won't leave like you came. Though I just found out the most horrible information, yet am I at peace. I don't know it all yet but I'm understanding it all better by and by. The four of us took a few pictures in front of the old house and we hit the road. The minute we pulled onto the Normandie traffic Aunt Nita spoke her word, "Lord, Here We Come. Now hit it in the ass, Chile, we got a lot of miles to put behind us, we don't owe this highway shit." Shelia and Remi just folded over in their seats laughing.

Our journey carried forward with pit stops and some antique shopping and we still arrived in town with good time. The trip gave me a chance to really get them up to speed on what to keep an eye out for and what to expect. When we made it to town I went straight to Ellis' to get updated on Lyles. Jayden was there awaiting my arrival. Ellis' smile could light all darkness. All of us staying at the grand house was our better decision. Considering that our new additions Shelia and Aunt Nita needed to stay sight unseen and a secret made the arrangement best. Naturally, Aunt Nita took on the role of being our matriarch, both she and Shelia fit right in without a hitch. Ellis upon first sight of Shelia grabbed her hands and began to do her thing. I saw her in the back corner of the great family room whispering words from the unknown to Shelia that both made her cry and rejoice. I just stood there taking the love all in. It felt great to be back in the fold of my crew but I needed to break free so that I could see the foundation.

From the outside things looked somewhat fine but when we entered the building I damn near collapsed. I knew that things would look bad but I wasn't expecting what I was seeing. Not only was there a fire but the place had been ransacked. I kept telling myself, Lucy, you got insurance and it's going to be alright. We can and we will rebuild. All will be well. By the time we got down near the closet where the bodies were found and past the crime scene tape both our phones were dinging with messages from Ellis. The identities of the two bodies were confirmed to have been Jill Ashley and Michael Bailey, two of my favorite AmeriCorps volunteers. They were just kids and their deaths weren't from the fire. Those bastards put bullets in their heads. It was all sad, but gunshot wounds to the head made my wheels start to spin. It didn't mean much in the grand scheme of things but I needed to know when the fire started.

"The fire report stated that the fire started around 11:30 p.m., right? Okay, Lyles wouldn't be here that late,

10:00 to the latest is his usual. Come, let's check all the entrances. This building would have been locked down by Lyles and I didn't notice any broken windows in our passing. I need to see how they got in. Just look around, all the cameras are intact. I'm willing to bet they killed the power to the building from the outside."

Sure enough that was the case. I started to run and laugh. Jayden couldn't figure it because he didn't see the full picture just yet. The server area in my office was a good starting point but it was destroyed as expected. Our culprit didn't discriminate. I began to laugh again.

"Now, Lucy, just wait just a good got-damn minute, what in the hell are you laughing about. These people have destroyed your building and used it as a murder scene. This is some serious shit. Come on, stop that damn laughing, girl. Talk to me!"

God, I need this to be right before I say a word to Jayden. Lyles' life sorta depends on it.

"Are you ready to go see Lyles at the county jail?"

"No, let's go to my house."

"Lucy?"

"Jayden, trust me on this, I think I can get to the bottom of this whole situation. Lyles will be just fine, they won't hurt him in there and he knows to keep quiet. Just trust me, let's get to my house."

We raced all the way back to my place so that I could log into the cloud for the backup footage but the system never had time to do the backup. There I was again shedding tears of sorrow. I cried harder than a newborn baby because I couldn't help but to keep thinking how all of this was my fault.

"Had I not started sticking my nose where it didn't belong the three would still be alive, those poor Americorp babies wouldn't be dead, maybe even Mrs. Ramirez would still be here and now they got Mr. Lyles. If not by the hand of God's mercy he'll be sentenced for murder and whatever comes with that and the man is innocent. I'm not God and I can't bear the whole world on my shoulders."

"This isn't your fault, Lucy. You, me and the whole gang know this to be true. We are going to get through this."

"But how?"

"I don't' know but we are going to make it. Repeat after me, 'We are going to make it!'"

"We are going to make it. We are going to make it! We are going to make it!"

"Girl, what you yelling for? God hears the still small voices."

I could chant this to the end of tomorrow but the not knowing what to do was driving me near nuts. It would seem that only God would know what to do in a time such as this. My granny used to sing ,"In times like this we need an anchor, in times like this we need the Lord." Truly we do need His touch.

"Well, let's get to the county jail."

"No, you were right. We don't need to go there. Lyles knows just want to do. We do need to find him a lawyer. Let's just go back to Schuster Hill and talk this thing through with the crew. We need to level this house up the best we can before the bricks really start to lean."

There's something about coming back to where you started empty handed that makes a failure a true fail. The whole way over I sat on the passenger side of his car quiet as a lamb waiting to be slaughtered. He was doing his usual words of inspiration but I kept pondering whether it was time to go to Marcelle and give in to his offer. The option to do or the option to die both shared a direct correlation with the true death. The blood on my hands flowed up and down my mind. I thought back to Uncle Jack and those boys. That was blood on my hands. I even felt like my parents' death added some as well. Had I come home a bit earlier ,just maybe they would still be here. Mrs. Ramirez, the volunteers and now Lyles is facing prison time. I feel like just one big cesspool of death and misfortune. I love this group of people, not just because they're all I have but I love them just because and I even love this little messed up community. Its home.. It seems to be full of misfortune for gentle souls, just ask the two volunteers or the three NOT hit by the train.

When we pulled onto the property in front of the house I heard just as clear as tomorrow "Enuff!" I looked over at Jayden, only I knew it wasn't his voice. Call me crazy but I knew it was Big Slim speaking to me. I didn't have to question it. Immediately the pity party stopped. I still can't say I knew what to do but there was hope. The how's and when's would fall into place. The kids were in the living room while the grown-ups sat in the foyer watching Ellis make the organ talk for Shelia. She was playing the music lowly but that old cooling board Leslie speaker was filling the room with rich sounds of peace. Aunt Nita sat there swaying to its sound.

"Did you guys find out anything?"

"No, I just needed to see where to begin with the foundation so I can get the insurance claim filed."

"Well, I spoke with Cousin Randy up in Little Rock, he's gonna come down and represent Lyles. He works up there at the Coronation Law Firm, one of the best firms in all the Delta."

"Can we trust Randy?"

159

"Yes, I would hope so. You know his daddy exiled him after he came out and Big Slim put that boy through college and law school. And do you know he repaid every cent back to her. His old daddy need his ass kicked from here to Jericho."

"I was a late teen around the last time I saw him.."

"Well stick around, he'll be here tonight."

The evening persisted while we talked and watched the children play and take naps. I joined Ellis in the kitchen with the food. I can't cook but I thought I could at least be useful. While she whipped up the meal we talked about my trip and then she began to speak words of encouragement in a low voice to keep the others out of it. Whispers of faith as Big Slim would call it.

After dinner I sat on the back porch alone looking off into the distance in the woods. Not thinking about any one particular thing. But then again the foundation and the children were on my mind. I considered the effects of the mere thought of my not reopening and just exiting the scene stage left. It wasn't long before my presence was joined.

"Oh, you're out here. Big Slim and me used to sit here for hours making sense of it all. Since she's been gone, I haven't been able to get a clear understanding. It's like I was robbed by a force I never saw coming. But look here, Lucy. What's really on your mind?"

"I just keep thinking how all of the secrecy, sneaking among the shadows and the smoking guns have led me to nowhere. Giving up seems like the best option. Y'all and all those worthy little kids back in town are what make the fight in my head struggle with walking away. Ellis, I just need a real break to get ahead of my enemy. I need my next move to be my best. Then there's the foundation, these folks went in there and did whatever the hell they wanted without so much as a conscience of who the real victims would be. They flat out didn't give a damn. If bad luck would have its way, Lyles and all his innocence will rot away in that damn cell because of me."

"Lucy, though the way seemeth dark, there is still plenty light for your path. I can't tell you the way to go but if you just calm down and speak to yourself the path itself will shine a bright light on the proper route. I am going to tell you this, ALL IS WELL. Go get yourself some rest. It'll all make sense in the morning."

What she said made sense. Indeed, I was tired, not so much physically but more along the lines of being defeated. Yet I sat there on the tinted window porch trying to relax my mind. But I kept traveling back to the Foundation and seeing those cameras. Surely, they could tell the story. But how and will it be on time?

Sometimes you have to bite the bullet and step into the ring with blood on your nose. I truly want to trust that all will be well, but too much is at stake. Just to sit back and let someone else guide the ship and hope for the best. I didn't want to do it again, but I need him and no matter how sadistic I think him to be somewhere behind the hysteria I know it comes from a place in love. I'm prideful and fearful but I'm not foolish, I know I can't put this star on the tree by myself. Me dialing his number from memory was the kicker. The brain knows even when it shouldn't.

"So you decided to call back? Going to hang up on me again or try and badger me some more for doing the necessary? Or did you want an antibiotic to try and cure the sickness of your existence for your little sanctum?"

"Look, let's cut to the chase. I am appreciative of all you've done and tried do over the years. I don't like what was done but it's done and over with. I don't forgive you for my parents."

"Marie, nobody regrets that day more than me, not even you my dear. I have tried to get some peace with it all over the years but it's all been a cheap bandage. Had I known our decisions would have led to their deaths maybe things would have been different. Now these thoughts are just vain repetition. We can only direct some of the future. I can't lose you too."

"I need your help. What do you know about Schuster Hill or the damn Schuster family?"

"I spent some time in Schuster Hill and Landing back when I first joined the league. Our job was to find out where children were going. But it only amounted to these poor souls trying to secure a meal for the bellies of their children. That Schuster Family Orphanage appeared to be a community godsend. The investigation came back positive and the file on the orphanage closed. But some years later I found out things were made to look that way. Old long-reaching money can make things conclude pretty quickly."

"I have in my possession a journal from Earnestos Beauteet, one of the boys that lived in the orphanage, his claim was that Ralph Schuster our current Mayor was molesting him and his mom was beating him."

"I don't remember the orphan but Little Ralph Schuster I do remember. I once caught him skinning a live cat. He indeed was a sadistic seeming little kid. I would have no doubt in believing he was raping those kids. Hell, his father the Mayor at the time was a natural sicko and believed in orgies and beating the hell out of his wife. She was nothing to pity though. That whole family was a problem but like I said we were made to believe peace was in the valley when in fact there was no peace. Only wealth and dark privilege."

"If only we could get in that house. Just maybe I could find something. I think the kids we have missing around town are locked away in there somewhere awaiting help."

"I wouldn't doubt that either. Rich people have this sense of entitlement to do whatever the hell they desire until they just can't. You be careful, Lucy, they will try to stop you if you start getting close."

"Too late on that one. My foundation was vandalized, burned and the plot for the murder of two of my volunteers and one of my friends here is being made to wear the blame. Actually, I called because I need you to come work your magic and help us through this situation."

"Not good. Not good at all. Why burn your place? Have you given them any cause to start retaliating? I wish I could come there but I've been wheelchair-bound for about six years now and I live in an assisted living facility. A bad car accident landed me here."

"Jesus, that's crazy. Why didn't you call? Never mind, you did call. I'm sorry, Uncle Jack. Well, I guess you can say I forced my way into this predicament about a year ago now. One of my students was taken and his mom called me the night of the incident. The mom died mysteriously in the middle of the same night. At the hospital no less. The boy's case was closed claiming he probably ran away to Mexico to his dad. And here recently the police chief got in my house and told me if I didn't play ball I would see life crumble all around me until I beg him to pull the trigger. I keep looking for a smoking gun but each time I crap out."

"Did your foundation totally burn and did it have cameras?"

"No and yes. I know where you're running but they killed the power of the building before entering and took the server. "

"Get those cameras off the walls, I'm willing to wager my wheelchair's right front wheel that those cameras have a backup battery pack installed for outages and they probably could be your smoking gun. Hell, they are your gun. Things aren't so mysterious these days. Help is in plain sight when you know what to look for. The blueprints of that Schuster house are likely to be on the national historic registry. Folks like this tend to take pride in relics of old history. And if memory serves me right there are some hidden entrance passages from an old library to the house. No, there was no sweet underground railroad fantasy. You need to know this, there's more than one evil in Schuster, as a matter of fact the true deal with the orphanage was mutilation sports and possible cannibalism of the poor. The Schuster's have been in dark dealings for years. Again never proven but highly suspected. Be careful and cling to your team at that funeral parlor. Their family business is much more than just a family business. Their bloodline and hands aren't totally clean but dirty money makes the world spin just as hard and fast as the clean."

The call ended but the CALL evolved.

That night I lay there in bed going in and out of alternate realities of what Jack said. Each time I awakened I felt the heaviness of the moment's burden. My mind felt stiff. My thoughts became contrary and too frustrating to even stomach. There were far too many thoughts and visions floating around my head. I needed peace, but I couldn't seem to stay asleep. Yet I declined walking the hallways of the house but I laid there in the dark trying to sift through it all. I didn't want to get my hopes up with the cameras, then I got to thinking about Mr. Lyles. All those times I called that man Mister Weird-ass and now he's sitting in prison because of me. The air was simply too damn thick to inhale.

All that pondering brought the suffering to my mind. There were just far too many what-ifs going into play for me to really rest through the night. I wanted to get up and walk the hallways like a tormented spirit caught between the veil. I really got to thinking over what Uncle Jack had said about these damn people eating children and tearing their bodies apart for sport. It was amazing that in my deep despair and wanting to start out fresh I would come to a community where he once lived. When I was a child Jack would tell me bedtime stories of a little town similar to this place that had characters like the wolf and Little Red Riding Hood and a group of townspeople fueled with greed and its power. I wish Big Slim were still here, this information would have been useful even just a few weeks ago. Funny how life plays out when we take the lead instead of following the natural flow.

By the time my alarm started to blare at 5:15 a.m. I could smell the infusion of a breakfast melody floating from room to room. Aunt Nita was indeed in the kitchen. Then came a slight knock on the door from Ellis to come join the population. I started to invite her in to ask if she remembered my Uncle Jack but then I digressed. This conversation would be best for another time.

"Rise and shine, Ms. Lucy, breakfast is ready."

"Thank you, I'll be down shortly."

Everyone was around the great table awaiting my arrival. When I took my seat, one of the kids invited grace, and the thanksgiving began.

"Lucy, did you sleep much last night?"

"No, not really, Ellis. I couldn't get my brain to shut down."

"I figured such because I heard you pacing the floor in your room. I was up too doing a bit of quilting. You could have come down for a spell. I have some tea that can cast down all worries."

"Cast down all worries? Ms. Ellis, child, what you be brewing? Some of that Mississippi moss? I'll be needing some of that before I return to the West."

"Miss Aunt Nita, what's Mississippi moss?"

"Honey child, it's some special jelly beans for adults." I thought her face would surely break from trying to hold in the laugh she had just created while trying to throw the child's minds off the herbal green's trail.

If the moment didn't already have laughter it really got funny when the children started begging for the jelly beans and telling which flavors they liked. The poor tykes had no idea what the adults were discussing. Ellis laughed so hard when little Julian said, "Mommy, I want some jellybeans too" She sprayed the poor child with orange juice.

"Miss Aunt Nita, you too much. Shelia, find yourself a corner and take Lucy too."

The remainder of the breakfast was filled with continuous laughter. We felt like one big happy family. After it was said and done Shelia and Ellis took the children to start class. Miss Aunt Nita as they called her went for a walk of the land to talk with God. I was left alone prepared to solve some mysteries. I got dressed and ready for the journey. I knew Jayden would be by shortly to pick herbs from Ellis' garden which would be perfect. When he got to the house and saw me standing on the porch the inner Scooby-Doo mystery incorporated must have been written all over my face because instead of getting herbs he said, "Come on, let's roll, Lucy." We used my car instead.

Along the ride he just sat there on the passenger side listening not saying much. I stopped and asked a couple times if something were the matter but each time he said no. I knew different but I also knew he would unfold at his own timing. We arrived, removed the main cameras and went to his place.

The old folks would say, "It's another day's journey. I'm so glad to be here." I don't disagree but nowadays I wonder what's so good about being here. We sifted through the cameras with such high hopes only to be let down yet again.

"I'm tired of this shit. Every time I get to breakthrough's door I find the bastard locked and welded shut. When am I going to able to walk on in?"

"Lucy, I'm right here with you, I just knew this was it. But let's not go into despair, we're gonna make it to the other side of this thing."

"Waking up on the other side of their favor is just what I'm worried about, Jayden. Who has to die or get framed next before this mess comes to a head? One of us could be next."

I sat there with no courage, damn near defeated. I hate to admit it but yet again they have the lead in this fight and I'm barely holding on with a fraying string.

"Well, I'm sorry again, Jayden, for wasting your time. I just need my branches to hold my weight for a change. All of this stuff is really getting next to me. It's like I've lost my direction for life. But let me get this stuff out of your way and get you back to your car."

"Come here, girl, let me hug all that fret away. I told you to stop worrying. Lucy, even strong titans like yourself have moments such as this. Pinch yourself, you're still human. In these moments you're either gonna fall and get back up or you're gonna fall and just wallow in defeat. Baby girl, you got a decision to make here and I know that you know how to solve this thing. So go for a walk, scream, shout, do whatever you got to do and meet me back up here this evening for dinner. Like I said there's another side to this coin and all we gotta do is flip it."

We departed presences but what he said stuck with me. I walked down the street to the park and decided to watch the ducks swim across the lake and exhaled right into some kind of vision.

Big Shelia and I watched Remi and Julian play on the slides and swings. I looked at my Big Shelia and she looked at me both with a smile. Smiles do a wonderful job of masking pain and its great frustration. Our smiles speak a language that no other can decipher but we two. It doesn't look good. It doesn't taste good. Nor does it even smell good, but it's gonna be all good. That's what my momma would say if she were here. In a moment's notice all the good in the world just left us.

"Aunt Lucy, I can't find Remi. His hiding spots are too good."

Lord God Almighty, tears filled my spirit, they've gotten my baby. The first thing I did was ran to the swing area looking for one of those damn foiled envelopes but I didn't see anything. We scattered around that park like a mange dog. We couldn't find him anywhere, this was so unlike him. I screamed his name like a mad banshee until my voice seemed to have stopped working. At this moment I saw my world flash before my eyes. Hell, it ended. All the moments I had planned and envisioned for his life passed me like a film. I wouldn't see him graduate high school nor college. He'd never get a chance to have a moment like this and call me for comfort. In this moment I knew Mrs. Ramirez's afflicting pain. The police arrived and were speaking with Shelia; she kept looking in my direction. Something deep within said run and I started running like my life depended on it. By the time I got close to the library I could hear what sounded like Remi crying. I knew it was all in my head but it didn't stop me from charging closer to the sound. I didn't have much voice left but I started yelling his name. "Remi baby, if you can hear Mommy, answer me, child!" I didn't know if this was an illusion from my sordid mind but I didn't give a damn. Finally, I coasted to the sound of my son to find him in the arms of Chief Marcelle who snapped his neck right in front of me. What I saw shattered any hints of humanity that remained within me. Red forms

170

took over my eyes. In a matter of seconds I was emptying the chamber into his lifeless corpse.

"Lucy! LUCY LUCY, wake up, girl!"

I could hear Jayden but I just thought he was looking around at the situation trying to stop me from executing justice on this low life.

"Girl, calm down, you done damn near destroyed this car. If you were this sleepy you should have caught a nap in the apartment. What the hell were you dreaming about?"

You couldn't ask for a better day It was all a nasty dream, but it kick-started my thinking.

"Those cameras need a power source!"

What's a dream without a nightmare? In the twinkling of an eye all things loved and gained can pass away. Today as we sit here for the start of the pre-trial, this fact really drives everything into perspective. We all are here to support our dear friend to justice. It is very uncomfortable to sit here and watch Lyles there beside Randy pretending to be strong. I don't have his feelings but I know there's got to be some uncertainty in his soul. In fact, each time the ole boy smiled in my direction his fear bled through. The truth he needed to know would overshadow his fear and open the eyes of the enemy. Though his pain be great I must keep quiet to save his soul. Too much was at stake so I prayed he and the gang would endure. Yet and still this truth didn't make it any easier to see him walked in the courtroom chained from hands to ankle like a common criminal. Each time Marcelle stood there at the head of the courtroom peering my way with that smile of his. He just knew deep down within that he had me in the thick of this pickle. After all, he practically guaranteed that I would regret the day I refused his offer. Smile now, you three-toothed bastard but you'll soon pay for these fears.

A jury of his peers sat before us on this first day. Randy thought it would difficult to make a jury selection in this community due to everyone knowing Lyles and the family. If everyone didn't already have the preconception that he was guilty this jury thing would not have been so difficult but having this insight Randy requested of the judge to have the case moved two counties north of Chicot County but the request was denied. A group of townsfolks was selected but not one minority was of the twelve. Just maybe the odds could have appeared balanced. Randy worked for the famed Coronation Law Firm in the big city but somehow the powers that be managed to fix it so his resources were limited and almost nonexistent in this case. He was allowed to represent Lyles as a sole practitioner with no backing from the firm. Yet again the reach of this evil hand was sweeping around the area like a storm cloud. As the process progressed the handsome young optimistic lawyer was catching hell but the little fella seemed determined. Since his arrival he'd sealed himself off from everyone to the library. I sometimes stand outside the door listening to him pacing and walking through his books of law. Everyone including the children seemed to be going through their coping mechanism during this troubling time. Keeping quiet was for the best, but even quiet time can be tiring.

The one thing I didn't keep between Jayden and I was that terrible vision from the park. In the midst of all things this truly worried me. The elders listened but not one had a word for its understanding, not even Ellis. Maybe had Aunt Nita not gone to visit her cousin down in Rodney, she might have had an inkling of understanding. Ellis just sat listening and then exited the room, for her comfort place, the kitchen. I think it was a general consensus that she went to check the meal that had teased our nostrils and made our taste buds water. Shelia just held my hand and extended her right hand up to the Father shaking it in silent praise. I felt her hand heat up while a single tear dropped from both her eyes. She whispered, "This thing ain't got no holt on the righteous. Devil, you got to let us go!" No other words were necessary and then off she went with the kids for their showers before dinner. Before following the other kids Remi ran to me with his little bear hug. Imagining that man with my son in his arms while snatching his last breath away made me hold tight to my baby. For the duration of this season that dream was all the motivation needed to continue to push forward with this journey. Victory shall be mine. They say little ones can see what adults can't and I believe my child can see. He scurried off up the stairs to join the gang. I sat there in the rocker looking out the window to the night's darkness almost void of thoughts.

"Lucy, that dream of yours, it felt real, didn't it?"

"Yes, ma'am, I woke up with the smell of my son's blood in my nose."

"Yes indeed, that was no dream, Lucy, it was a vision. You can't hang around seers and not expect to start seeing the other sides of things. I had a vison the other day myself, I was in a room similar to a basement hearing chains rattle and the sounds of children crying. Funny thing is I know the place but I just haven't pinned it down. Lucy, I don't know if this is hopeful thinking or God speaking but Lyles is going to be released of this hell and the captives are gonna be set free. Whatever way you want to look at it God is going to see us through to the end of this thing. And you know something else, you got a crown to wear. Just keep with it, Lucy, and don't worry about that vision, it only came to pull the covers off your eyes. When I woke up this morning I said it's another day's journey and Sister I'm so glad to be here!"

At the close of the day she got on the organ and played a bit of encouragement for the whole group with that very saying. She was on to something with everything being alright and I believe that God trusts us to make it through. Even He knows this game has to be played and executed in a righteous but deadly way.

Last night I dreamed. You know how in the dream world you become one with the spirit so it's understood that you are here, there and everywhere at the same time. There I stood in the foundation before the fire. Standing at the entrance was Mayor Ralph Schuster and Chief Marcelle looking in my direction like vultures. They worked as a pair trashing the place until they reached that closet. They opened the door and the sound of two shots echoed through the halls. Upon opening the door I saw it was me laid over in the corner with a bullet wound to the head. I guess the realization must have scared me out of my sleep. I woke up sweating profusely. I don't claim to understand all these dreams. Some have a meaning but other times they are just apparitions of what I might have previously thought or spoken. The insurance adjustment check has been placed on hold until the trial is over and it's made clear that I'm not connected to the fire at all. Without those funds there is no way possible for me to even begin to make any of the repairs necessary to get the place back up and running. Randy is expecting the trial to be over in three days but the kid's pretty nervous about winning. It's been said around town that the prosecution is pulling all the stops, to make this thing airtight.

Today was the first day of the actual trial. As we entered the courtroom there stood the Mayor and Chief Marcelle surrounded by the media. Giving interviews I lingered there while the Mayor spoke, claiming that as mayor one of his biggest responsibilities is protecting his people and that he couldn't do anything of this nature without Chief Marcelle.

"Chief Marcelle. What can you tell us about this case?"

"Well the most I can say is justice will definitely be served. This man tortured those two innocent souls, then murdered them, placed them in a closet and shut the door. Then he came back, doused their bodies with gasoline, struck a match and closed that closet door again as if he had just finished taking out the trash. Thankfully, we have two eyewitnesses not afraid to come forward in speaking the truth. Justice is definitely around the corner it will prevail."

"Will the death penalty be sought in this case?"

He looked in my direction with that slight grin he permanently wears and continued answering the reporters' questions. In fact, he and the Mayor looked into my eyes long enough to try and make me aware of who was in control. I couldn't take it anymore, so I joined the others inside. Making it inside just in time to see Lyles brought out. His face appeared swollen on the right side in the eye area. I rushed to Randy. Lyles whispered something to him.

"Lucy, it was just a misunderstanding in the shower. He's fine and we'll make sure it doesn't happen again."

He answered me but I could read his annoyance to my presence. This immediately called his loyalties into question. I took my seat with the gang while the proceedings began. It started out strong with the defense giving his spiel and then the prosecutor David Meeks threw in his bone. He and I somewhat dated maybe two years ago. I remembered the arrogant prick took me to dinner and on the ride back home thought a steak, a little lobster and some expensive wine was the key to unlocking this girl's chastity. Needless to say we've not been fans of each other since that time. A rather unfortunate feat for this present time. By the time they got to the questioning it seemed like this guy had a playbook of all the right questions intended to defame Lyles' now fragile character. No rock went unturned. While Randy seemed to be struggling to even do his job. I just couldn't figure it. I've watched this joker for weeks rehearsing this case. Albeit he was home in the comforts of himself and the mirror but still this man is better than what he is displaying to us today. Again my suspicions heightened. At the rate we are going this trial won't make it past tomorrow. Call me crazy but something ain't right and I know where to look this time.

I excused myself to the restroom but hightailed it back to the house. There was sure to be about an hour and a half more points of badgering which gave me plenty of time to find what I was sure to find.

What I saw in his room confirmed it all. This fella was not a trial or criminal defense attorney, he was a tax and estate planning attorney but that wasn't even the worst of it. He had a copy of the Schuster Hill estate deed and that of someplace called the House under his mattress. This house place had Big Slim's name and heirs listed as the benefactors of the property. Maybe it's referring to this house but fortunately there was a parcel number listed and upon cross-checking it online I saw yet another shot that should have been heard around the world. The house place was the old Schuster Orphanage better known as the Mayor's home. This document listed Big Slim as the benefactor over 25 years ago. This kid isn't here to help us, he's here to ruin us from within! My phone started to ring; it was Jayden.

"Hey, Lucy, where you at?"

"Had to use the restroom, what's up?"

"Well, we are on recess and Randy says that the prosecution is willing to offer a deal. And he thinks Lyles should consider it because things don't look good for him in there, Lucy."

"No! No deals. Get in there with Lyles and tell him no. Where is Ellis? You guys get to Lyles. Randy isn't who he says he is and he sure as hell isn't trying to defend Lyles. I'm on my way, get back in there!"

The time for the truth to shine is now.

It was my plan to do this in a more eloquent way but with his lifeline at stake there was no time for semantics. There were about five news station crews on the steps of the courtroom. Thanks to Darryl I had a bag full of flash-drive copies ready for the kill. Still, I didn't want them to know who was dropping the bombshell. When I drove on the scene, I saw the crowd but I didn't see my way to the finish line. I sat there in the car silently praying for the light to my pathway. Then it all became clear. Across the street were kids I didn't recognize playing basketball. Today must have been a teacher's workshop day or something. Now I needed just one unlikely kid to fit the part. Not being able to pinpoint my groundbreaker, I got out and walked in their direction. Being teenage boys they never gave me a second glance. I was fully clothed and not twerking. I damn near walked that court overlooking for my little shepherd boy and had just about given up when I found a young man sitting to himself on a bench outside the court talking to his opponents on a video game. While he had his head down and I approached slowly, but quick to see the error in my judgment. I didn't need what appeared to be a quiet timid kid but I rather I needed a young hustler. I turned and walked right in the middle of the play towards the guy doing the most talking and swearing. Everyone just paused at my presence. Some of the kids started to yell but my guy cut all the noise quickly with the wave of his hand.

"Dude shut up and respect your elders. Nobody ever taught you how to treat a lady? Yes, ma'am, where would you like me to sign? Come come, let's step into my office."

He was indeed the charmer I needed for this job.

"Afternoon, sir. I'm Lucy and I got a job I'm sure hoping you can handle."

He threw the ball back to the gang and they were back at it without missing a beat. I saw the dollar signs he saw written all over me as we walked over in the direction of the gamer kid. I wanted to keep this as delicate as possible, so I was a bit uneasy around the gamer but small world-ish and coincidental that young lad was his 10-year-old brother Jason.

"That's my little brother. He has his head stuck in that game; he wouldn't hear you screaming his name over a bullhorn. My name is Daniel, so what's this job you have? Now I can't be doing anything illegal, me and my brother were just placed here from the system and I can't get separated from him. We're all we got."

Damn, here I am placing yet another person in harm's way. But it's gotta be done.

"It's not illegal but it is serious. Really all I need you to do is drop something off with those news crew people across the street. But it needs to be done carefully."

"Does it have something to do with that Mr. Lyles case?"

"Yes it does. You know Lyles? Didn't you say you just moved here?"

"Yes, we just moved here with my Aunt Pringlaye. She owns the bakery on Main Street. You know her, she sells the crack sandwiches?"

This was suddenly starting to hit a bit too close to home. Pringlaye is the mouth of the South. She tells everything and I don't know her loyalty level. But at the same time I don't want to put this kid at risk, but I need it done.

"Ma'am, did you say your name is Lucy? Not by chance the Lucy that runs the foundation that Mr. Lyles got framed in?"

"Yes, I'm she."

He said, "If what you got is gonna help I'll do it for free. I overheard my no-good aunt and the mayor discussing this case just yesterday. I didn't hear it all, but I know it ain't right. Just tell me what to do. We got to save this Mr. Lyles, they're planning to have him locked up for life and the man is innocent."

I texted Jayden for the Chief and the Mayor's whereabouts. Confirmed that they were in the courtroom. We had a five-minute window to execute this plan. I handed him the flash drives with 500 in cash and watched him work his magic. I even stood there with his little brother till I saw him coming back cross the street. The news crews started racing off the scene. I felt accomplished in my deed, but I had one more shot to fire, District Attorney Deedee Banks. This I would drop off in person.

The D.A. office appeared empty as a ghost town. There was not one soul lingering in the front office. The phones went unanswered. I could see everyone standing in the glass-walled conference room. With no one to stop me I ventured to this area but not inside. From the outside I witnessed my handiwork being not only visualized on the TV but also being heard. The four news crews each received footage from one of the four camera angles in the foundation. Each had been shared with this office. Things really reached a climax when it came to those two poor souls. Chief Marcelle showed no mercy in shooting both in the head execution-style. They were made to get on their knees and watch as plastic bags were taped over their heads. In between begging for mercy they struggled to breathe until the lethal shots were fired into their skulls. Their lifeless bodies collapsed to the floor and then were dragged to the broom closet where they were positioned and doused with gasoline. From what my teary eyes could see the room contained not a single dry eye.

DeeDee shut the TV off and when she turned around our eyes locked. I imagine we mutually shared the look of hell, one for injustice and the other for the shame. My only interest in coming to this place was to see her face. This lady spoke so highly in regard to seeking a life sentence for Lyles because as she guaranteed the public, he was a meticulous ruthless murderer. I wonder how it felt on the inside to know the two men you have worked tirelessly with and regarded so highly all these years are in fact actually shameless murderers. But the epiphany of those raw emotions was neither here nor there, I just needed my friend exonerated and set free of the charges.

I was halfway back to my car when my cell phone started buzzing, text messages were coming from the crew but the first one was from Uncle Jack.

"Congrats, Lucy, you cracked this thing wide open, I couldn't have done it any better."

There were quite a few more text messages chiming through, but I opted not to read them. I had my mind on getting back to the courtyard to see it all unfold before my very own two eyes. The news crews were back this time in what appeared to be double the cars. I made it just in time as four FBI agents were walking the Mayor and Chief down the steps of the courthouse. Somehow, I managed to get to the head of the crowd so that the two lowlifes could see my face. We three locked eyes for a brief moment before the shots were heard. The crowd dropped to the ground, yet I stood there frozen in disbelief watching as both the Chief and the Mayor lay toppled on the concrete no doubt gasping for their last breaths. I don't know what made me do it, but I rushed to the side of the Chief and grabbed hold of his hand. The agents were trying to push me back and almost managed to do so. Not before he had a chance to tell me what he couldn't earlier, as in his last breath he had whispered, "He has the children."

181

I sat there on my knees in front of his void body. Not concerned with the noise of the scattering crowd. All of my plotting and scheming was now over. These men were dead and so were their secrets. I'll never have my day in court with them. I don't get the sweet victory of triumphing on their names, all of those glories ceased to exist rather too quickly. So many tails have been left untucked. The world got silent to my awareness and I got to thinking where would he, assuming the Mayor was the mystery He, be hiding some children? Quick thinking brought Randy to mind. There was still yet some sting available for him, but we needed him to help us go through the mansion. I heard my name in the distance, but my focus couldn't recourse to the direction of the caller. It wasn't until Jayden and Ellis were both right in front of me, all hands on deck, that I became lucid enough to speak. I didn't see Randy but I needed to speak quick and quiet.

"Guys, those children are in that old mansion. We can't trust Randy but we might need his guidance."

"Well, that's where we need to go but how with all these police now involved?"

"Ellis, the house belongs to you. I found a document in Randy's room that proves it. He was working with the Mayor to somehow forge your claim off that old will."

"We need to get in there before the FBI gets there. Their story doesn't just stop here with their deaths."

We all agreed but then the path became clear when Jayden dangled the Mayor's keys in his hand.

As we quickly faded from the scene and into the crowd I glanced back over my shoulder to see the shooter being laid face down on the cold pavement. It was shocking to see that it was the water clerk Ms. Humbreye. I just had to stop and see this in real-time. The woman took being subdued like it was nothing to it. There were no tears, while the police Mirandized her, she kept reciting "I eliminated the threat! I eliminated the THREAT!". No lie there, she did that but just too soon. I couldn't figure the angle ,but it'll all come out in the wash this we can be sure. In turning to rejoin the gang I was surprised to see they still stood there behind me equally shocked. Ellis lifted and pointed her hand in the direction of Ms. Humbreye. God only knows the mighty prayer of grace that hand spoke to the Throne. Shortly we were pulling up to the backside of the library and while sitting in the back seat of the Cadillac the rational reality of it rushed into our minds like that of a mighty flood.

"Guys, we can't enter that house by ourselves. Who knows what or who could be waiting for us. Let's go back for those agents."

"We can't trust the FBI with this," said Jayden.

"I know. But we need some form of police in this. We cannot enter that place without the law near us. But let me think."

"I got it, let's get Eugene here with us. Come on, let's think through this logically. Okay, he has that file about the three and though nothing ever became of it, I know the boy's eyes became wide open. No, he never mentioned it to me but he now wears the look."

"What look?"

"Lucy, he had the look of being WOKE. So what do you say? Do we call him or not? Before you say anything I want to continue living and I don't want to be sitting in no damn jail cell doing it either."

Everyone agreed that calling Eugene would be best. Jayden worked the show and got him to the library parking lot. The kid had this sober look on his face. I could tell from the puffiness of his eyes he had been crying. Though my tears were under lock and key in regard to those two bastards I understood his position and proceeded to embrace the dear soul with a hug, but when I got near he snatched back in anger.

"You people played a game of God and humanity. Never once thought twice about my life while you commanded the roles either. You put my life in jeopardy with that file and I know one of you did it."

Jayden and I just stood there solemnly looking with no words between us for this situation.

"I considered you two to be my friends but yet you weren't. I get it you didn't know who to trust. But hell, just because they're dead doesn't mean you can remove the firewall now, does it? I got the answer for you. No, it doesn't. I don't know what you guys even have in mind but I got a small child and wife to get back home to today. I'm not in this fight. I wish you the best but I'm out. The most I can do is give you this."

He handed us three radios with red and yellow buttons on top.

"I'm disappointed in you guys but I still care. I know y'all. I'm sure everybody is packing, so firepower won't be a problem. These radios have heightened frequency chaser capabilities. That place is fortified, no cell will work beyond the main floor. I don't know what you guys will find but I know you'll find something that I just can't be a part of. At any rate the red button will alert and pinpoint your location

184

to the authorities within a 50-mile radius of this place. Use it only when absolutely necessary. The yellow is for your communication purposes. I put all four radios on a private frequency so no worries of the wrong person listening in."

"You only gave us three radios."

"I have the fourth. I'll do what I can from afar, but I can't be tied in with you rebels. Now go and be safe. I'll you know what's happening out here when the time comes. Oh yeah, one more thing, when this shit is all over, I want a full explanation and free family meals for a year, Jayden."

His request was fair and accepted.

When we got back in the car Ellis was scoffing at her phone and showing its screen in all our directions. It was Randy. I know he wanted our 10-20 but that couldn't be revealed.

"Tell him we're gone to Rodney to get the children cupcakes at the Cake Factory. I'm always raving about their blueberry donuts and sweet treats, he's sure to buy that one. As a matter of fact, Ellis, just text him. Tell him to meet us at the house, we'll be there in an hour. Ask him what his favorite flavor is."

While she was handling that bit of information, I made Shelia aware of the situation. She thought it would be best to gather the children to go see a movie and get some ice-cream. The kids definitely deserved an outing, and with God's help, all will be well He texted Ellis back… "Surprise Me." Indeed, his surprise was coming quicker and brighter than he'd ever expected.

The wail of the sirens drew closer and closer. In almost a twinkling of the eye the Mayor's house was surrounded by police and FBI agents. Our plan was fouled before we ever got a chance to carry it out. We sat there in the car watching them force their way through the twin front doors. Soon three people were escorted out of the house. We continued to wait patiently for the children to come running out like wild horses but after 20 minutes there was no presentation of little ones. In thinking about what Eugene said about the radios it was understood that it would probably be a while before they got around to the area where the children might be. Some twenty to twenty-five agents entered the estate, so we took great comfort in knowing that they would find and liberate the children. After waiting for what seemed like an eternity in the time of patience the agents exited the building and allowed the three workers to return back inside the estate. In all this time we didn't exchange any words but rather we sat eagerly awaiting to see Ellis' dream of twenty children being released from the confines of this hell. Instead, the dream didn't come to reality. I kept wondering to myself if not here, where? The feeling of defeat spread within the car like the black plague though we were disappointed and utterly disgusted with the whole situation, we stayed in our position until the last agent exited the scene and the three workers left the grounds. The front door was secured and taped off like a crime scene with one of our local cops left out front as a guard. God, I just don't understand why we can't catch a real break and enjoy the freefall of it all. With each attempt comes an epic fail it seems. This situation seems like a bucket of crabs. If even one gets nearly to the top 50, others reach out to yank him back down to the bottom. Like I have been saying since day one this mess just gets stranger with each moment and, in the process, has made me strange too. We left the back parking lot for the road back to my car when Eugene called Jayden's cell.

"Hey, man, where are y'all?"

"Just pulled out from the library parking lot."

"I'm walking out of the library now. We need to sit down and discuss this thing. Without that lawyer friend of y'alls."

"Come to the shop. Me, Lucy and Ellis will be there."

"Cool, I'll see you guys in 15 minutes. Bring Mr. Lyles, he can definitely help with this."

We all locked eyes. Caught up in the fervor of this situation Mr. Lyles got far from our minds.

"Bailiff said it would take a few hours to get all his release paperwork completed. I told him to call me the minute he is released. So, we're good, come on, let's get to my apartment."

I wondered what door God had cracked for us this time around. We entered the building from the backside to make sure to not run into Pringlaye or any other undesirable. Just as his word declared the phone started to ring. It was Eugene needing to be brought upstairs to the apartment. While Jayden went to bring him up, Ellis and I got a moment to talk.

"Lucy, I just want to thank you for being a part of our lives. Something down deep within me tells me this thing is just about finally over. We are gonna find those children alive and well and we are going to do our damnedest to make their lives normal again. So you stop sitting there worrying your little self to death. This thing is almost over, Lucy…it's almost done. The good Lord didn't bring us this far to leave us."

"Thank you for being my friend, Ellis. Without you and your family I wouldn't have made it to this point. I would have been gone or probably dead long before now. I know it's all going to work out, Ms. Ellis. I am going to hold on, don't you worry none about that. "

We sat holding our hands in comfort and were quite surprised to see Lyles enter the room. It'd only been a few weeks but it sure felt like years had passed since I last saw my friend. Ellis and I ran and grabbed hold of him like he was a million bucks. We almost hugged the life out of his strong frame. I know I had been saying that everything was going to be alright but now I knew for sure everything is going to be alright. Soon Jayden and Eugene entered the room with rolls of maps in hand and a plan from the heart in their eyes.

"Okay, I got to thinking when I left you guys. For years I had heard there was some strange juju happening with the Mayor and that the Chief was in on it. But like most rumors it died off. But then these kids would disappear and like always the case would conveniently be closed by the Chief as border returns. Always Mexican kids. Like I say, when I left you guys I hoped you all would find something but the Feds made you fall short. So I went back to City Hall for building permit records on the mansion and stopped by the library for the blueprints of the original house since it's on the registry."

"Okay, you said all this to say what, Eugene?" Jayden asked.

"Isn't it obvious, Jayden, the Feds didn't find any children because the house has been fortified and altered. If you don't know what you're looking for, plain sight stuff will get passed over. Come on, roll those plans out, Eugene. The boy at the library told me there used to be a passage between the library and the old mansion through the basement of the library. And I bet it's still available."

Looking at his watch Jayden said, "That's all fine and dandy but the library is closed."

"No worries. I clean the library and I think I have that key in my belongings bag from the prison," said Lyles.

We rummaged through the plans and blueprints for the way. Soon we had it all laid out. It was decided that Jayden and Ellis would return home to deal with Randy and his shenanigans. I felt confident that Jayden would be there just in case he tried anything crazy. As handy as Ellis was with her gun he'd better hear her words and scurry his little rinky-dink self on down the road. We waited till first dark to make our move to the library. With Lyles knowing the place well it was a no brainer to have him come with us.

Just to think I sat on the floor of this building's basement reading with no hints or indications available for me to even imagine that I was sitting at the entrance to some soul's hell. A makeshift closet packed with boxes of old books merely stood between those children and me. This little area might have had about 20 to 25 boxes stacked or packed in the way of the other door but with three hungry soldiers on the loose there wasn't a box in the world able to keep us from it. The door was cobwebbed sealed without the hint of a lock. Behind it reeked of dampness but overall its character shined through brightly. The ground and walls were foundation-ed with bricks similar to that of the late 1800s. It was a straight shot to wherever the hell it would lead us. Best of all no rats in sight.

In steps of maybe 150 we found ourselves at the end of the line to the door that opened to a solid wall. Not a brick wall but a regular studded wall of sheetrock, it meant nothing to Eugene as he put his size 13 boot right through it like a sheet of wrapping paper and used his body like a sledgehammer through the remaining material where we landed in the basement of the old mansion. Nothing in particular stood out about the room other than it appeared rather small. A little too small for the taste of our Mayor. Even more so different about the place was it was completely empty. I just stood there leaning on the wall with my eyes closed listening to the guys talk. While they spread the blueprints on the floor reviewing for the direction I continued leaning on that wall while Lyles tried recollecting the placement of the room from his childhood.

"Indeed this is the right place but the basement wasn't always boxed in like it is now. In fact, from the specs the basement mimics the whole house in size. Lucy, try pressing around on that wall for a trapdoor or something. If not Eugene and them boots don't mind making a way." He said almost in tears.

Sure enough along the seam of the wall gave way to movement. It in fact rotated judging from the rub abrasions on the floor but it seemed to be stuck. Again nothing for the might of Eugene's boot. No doubt from the noise what was behind this wall of affliction was startled. My God, what this fallen wall opened to was dreadful and almost holy. The sound of rasped cries and hopeless moans filled the soundwave. I stopped dead in my tracks when I heard those sounds of frustrating fear. I thought for a moment on had we not come this way, what would have become of these detained people. It's bad enough that they were kidnapped and held here against their will but to be left here to starve was just too much for my mind to process. The place was set up with six doors on both sides of the wall and at the end of the hallway was the main door that led to something I didn't need to see. It was some sort of playroom with cameras, nothing too sadistic there I guess if only that's the full extent of this site.

The hallway was white but each of the doors was glass and assigned a rug that was color-coded in pairs of green, red, and blue with the door at the end of the hallway appearing whiter than the walls. There appeared to be no locks on the doors, only a handle on both sides. At the first door I saw who I vowed to find. It was him, I could hardly believe my eyes! God, I wish his mother were here today. I screamed his name and bolted to the door. He jumped out of bed and screamed, "Ms. Lucy, NO!"

Man, let me tell you, getting hit by a lightning bolt ain't no game nor claim to fame. I don't know how much time had passed in between reviving me but when I did come around all eyes were on me.

"Ms. Lucy are you okay?" said Raphael.

I looked around and saw what had been a source of doom and gloom now replaced with concern and happiness.

Those children each stood at the gate of their hell wearing smiles on their otherwise distressed faces. They probably imagined this day would come no nearer to them than a distant dream.

"I guess I'm fine, guys. Don't worry, I'll be more careful. I'm okay. Let's see about getting you out of this hell hole. Any idea how we can do that?"

The voice of what sounded like a male adult spoke up from the far end of the hallway.

"He usually brings this little remote and chooses the mat color and number and opens it. It's on the wall there in that room at the end. We've all seen it but none have been fortunate enough to gain such a save."

I scooted up against the wall after assuring Lyles and Eugene I was fine. They scurried down the hallway carefully to the room at the end of the hall. Though I was anxious to release the children; I was greatly comforted in knowing they would all be returning to their families. Well not exactly all. I sat there smiling at Raphael while he smiled so brightly back at me. He asked me a thousand questions and I had the answers until he brought up his mom.

"Ms. Lucy, I can't wait to see my mom. I just want to hug her tight. How's she been doing?"

The time had been great since his disappearance. I really hated to break this kid's heart. I sat there smiling but I dropped my head when I felt the tears forming in my eyes. I had the words but just didn't want to force them from my lips. But I couldn't have this poor baby stepping one foot from this hell and not know the real truth. He deserved it. Hell he earned the truth. So, although the electric shock had me a little dazed and weak, I mustered the strength to both stand and speak while yet leaning on that wall.

"Raphael, listen, child, your dear mother is no longer with us. She passed shortly after you went missing."

He just stood there for a moment and said nothing. Then the poor baby turned and collapsed on the bottom bunk of his bed. Though he was surely heartbroken the child didn't shed a tear. I imagined being here in this sort of hell for so long made all other things the lesser evil and worth no tears. Standing there equally quiet I searched for the right thing to say or to even feel for that matter. What do you tell a kid that's been taken against his will and held in bondage for what seemed an eternity and when the time comes for him to be released from this hell, in what should be the happiest moment of his life, you crush him with bad news? I don't know how to make this thing better.

"Sweet baby, I can't imagine how you feel right now. I promised your mother that I would be here for you, sweet child. Don't you worry about a thing, I'll see that you get all the help you need. When we get you all out of here, I got a place for you in my home. It's okay to cry, baby. The destruction of this world ain't the sort of thing you get used to; you just learn to deal with it."

He didn't say a word either way; God, didn't I feel useless. The men were still away rummaging around looking for that magic remote. I stood there looking for a way to make a difference. Then I remembered something my mom would say: "most times the way to escape looks you right in the face." I thought quickly to retrace my steps back into the main basement area. Like she said, it was there, the breaker boxes. He was anal enough to label the boxes, fortunately. The box I needed was labeled 'dungeon' of all things. I flipped the one main switch and heard the sweetest sound of locks disengaging.

"Okay, fellas, I took the first shock, one of you two strong men check the doors!" I yelled back through the torn wall.

While the fellas didn't hear me the kids took the chance and were standing in the hallways laughing, crying and embracing. I don't know how much religion they had been fed prior to this time but whether they knew it or not those babies were praising God. Lyles and Eugene appeared with the magical remote with a "what the hell" look on their faces. All couldn't get any better, every child was accounted for except Raphael. I looked in his holding cell and he lay there in the fetal position quiet as a lamb. I ushered for the others to go on. Aunt Nita's saying came to mind "Lord here we come", I definitely needed his touch.

"Baby boy, why aren't you out with the others celebrating?"

"Ms. Lucy, I dreamed about this moment a million times over. Believe it or not I knew you would find me. But now that the moment is here and my mom's gone, I feel like it's all for not. I don't have nobody. Those guys out there hopefully still have their families to return to but I'm an orphan now. My daddy is dead and my mommy is dead. Ain't nobody gonna love me like my mom."

"You must not have heard a word I said earlier. You're my family now if you want to be and God knows I really want you to be my family, Raphael. My Remi needs a big brother just like you and I need you too. So what do you say, will you join our family?"

"Ms. Lucy, I'm damaged but I'm willing."

His hug made all the pain and frustration seem like a melted snowflake. We walked out of that wretched place from the front door. Eugene had made some calls. The FBI, the police, the news stations and the world seemed to have sprawled outside those doors with expectations of a High King's arrival. The existence of the lost years faded in the backgrounds of their carrouseling lives. Indeed, the true Wolves had finally come out from the wilderness and are no longer Lost on the Way Home.

We hope you enjoyed reading this JP Productions Book.

Thanks for reading. If you enjoyed this book, please consider leaving an honest review on Amazon.com.

Visit our website below and subscribe to the mailing list. Once you join our mailing list exclusive updates on new releases, promotions and more will be delivered right to your inbox.

JPWRITESPRODUCTIONS.COM/MAILING-LIST